THE CALL

Praise from Bestselling Authors

"Michael Grant has concocted a hilarious adventure with *The Magnificent 12*. Pretty much every line made me smile or chuckle—it's laugh-out-loud funny—which is really saying something since it's about a kid who has to save the world from destruction. It's a *Monty Python*–like invasion of middle school that keeps you turning pages just to know what the young hero will say next."
—D. J. MacHALE, author of the Pendragon series

"Welcome to *Monty Python* meets *The Lord of the Rings*. The future of all civilization rests in the hands of a middle school wimp with more phobias than muscle groups, and saving the world has never been funnier."
—GORDON KORMAN, author of *Pop, Zoobreak*, and two books in the 39 Clues series

"Fantastically funny and fast-paced, *The Magnificent 12* is written with a dry wit and a wonderful economy of words."
—ANGIE SAGE, author of the Septimus Heap series

"A thrill ride through time with cool monsters, relatable heroes, *and* big laughs. What more could a kid ask for?"
—PATRICK CARMAN, author of the Land of Elyon series, the Atherton Trilogy, and Skeleton Creek series

Also by Michael Grant

Gone
Hunger
Lies

MICHAEL GRANT

BOOK ONE

THE CALL

KATHERINE TEGEN BOOKS
An Imprint of HarperCollins*Publishers*

Katherine Tegen Books is an imprint of HarperCollins Publishers.

The Magnificent 12: The Call
www.harpercollinschildrens.com

Library of Congress Cataloging-in-Publication Data
Grant, Michael.
    The call / Michael Grant. — 1st ed.
        p.   cm. — (The Magnificent 12)
    Summary: A seemingly average twelve-year-old learns that he is destined to
gather a team of similarly gifted children to try to save the world from a nameless
evil, which is threatening to reappear after having been imprisoned for three
thousand years.
    ISBN 978-0-06-183366-3
    [1. Fantasy.   2. Adventure and adventurers—Fiction.   3. Good and evil—
Fiction.   4. Humorous stories.]   I. Title.
PZ7.G7671Cal   2010   2009044815
[Fic]—dc22   CIP
                                                                        AC

Typography by Amy Ryan
10   11   12   13   14   LP/RRDB   10   9   8   7   6   5   4   3   2   1
❖

First Edition

For Katherine Tegen,
who believed I could be funny.

And for Katherine, Jake, and Julia,
who still aren't sure.

BOOK ONE

THE CALL

One

David MacAvoy—whose friends called him Mack—was not an unlikely hero. He was an *impossible* hero.

First, there was the fact that he was only twelve years old.

And then there was the fact that he was not especially big, strong, wise, kind, or good-looking.

Plus he was scared. Scared of what? Quite a list of things.

He had arachnophobia, a fear of spiders.

Dentophobia, a fear of dentists.

Pyrophobia, a fear of fire, although most people have some of that.

Pupaphobia, a fear of puppets. But he was not afraid of clowns, unlike most sensible people.

Trypanophobia, a fear of getting shots.

Thalassophobia, a fear of oceans, which led fairly naturally to selachophobia, a fear of sharks.

And phobophobia, a fear of phobias. Which makes more sense than it may seem at first because Mack was always finding new fears. And it scared him to have more scary things to be scared of.

Worst of all, the horror among horrors: Mack had claustrophobia, a fear of cramped spaces. A fear, to put it as unpleasantly as possible, of being buried alive.

So this was not a twelve-year-old you'd expect to become one of the greatest heroes in human history— not the person you'd expect would try and save the world from the greatest evil it had ever faced.

But that's our story.

One thing to remember: most heroes end up dead.

Even when they don't end up dead themselves, people around them very often do.

Mack was an okay-looking kid: crazy, curly brown hair; medium height; medium build. He had a serious case of mediumness.

His eyes were brown, too, which is the most common eye color in the world. But there was something else about his eyes. They were eyes that noticed things. Mack didn't miss much.

He noticed how people looked at him, but he also noticed how they looked at each other and how they looked at things, and even how they looked at a printed page.

He noticed details of how people dressed, how they moved, how they spoke, how they trimmed their fingernails, and how they held their book bags. He noticed a lot.

This habit of noticing things was very useful when it came to Mack's hobby, which was provoking bullies and then fleeing from them.

Just five days before Mack learned that he was going to have to save the world, he was first concerned with saving himself.

Mack attended Richard Gere Middle School in Sedona, Arizona. (Go, Fighting Pupfish!) The school was blessed in a number of ways, but cursed in others. It was known to have a number of excellent teachers. It had advanced placement yoga classes, and something called noncompetitive bowling was an elective.

It also had more than its share of bullies, which meant that the bullies had to organize. The bullies at RGMS each had his or her own sphere of influence.

The jocks had a bully, the skaters had a bully, the prep/fashionistas had a bully. The stoners had a bully, but he tended to lose focus and so was not very effective at terrorizing people. The nerds had one bully and the geeks had another. Even the goth kids had a bully, but he was out with mono so the emo bully was filling in.

But there was one bully to rule them all, one bully to find them, one bully to bring them all and in the darkness pound them. And this bully was Stefan Marr.

Like Mack, Stefan Marr was in seventh grade. Unlike Mack, he was fifteen.

Stefan was big, blue-eyed, blond, and handsome.

And he was terrifying.

Stefan was not academically gifted. Let's just put it that way because the alternative way of putting it might be rude. But he was fearless. While Mack had twenty-one identified phobias, Stefan had zero. In fact, you could say his number of phobias was in the negative numbers because there were some scary things that even completely normal people avoided that Stefan went looking for.

When Stefan would see a sign that read, "Beware of Dog," he would interpret that to mean "come on in."

On this particular day, a Wednesday in October, Mack would have a run-in with Stefan that would change both of their lives.

The problem had started with Horace Washington III, a kid Mack kind of knew and kind of liked, who was being introduced to the concept of a swirlie. Horace was a nerd, and therefore the swirlie was being administered by Matthew Morgan, the bully for nerds. Matthew was ably assisted by his frequent partner, Camaro Angianelli. Camaro had never gotten over being named after her father's favorite car, and she expressed her sensitive nature by bullying geeks.

Strictly speaking, Camaro should not have been in the boys' bathroom at all, but the last person who had pointed this out to her now ate his meals through a straw.

In any event, Matthew and Camaro had Horace upended. His head was in the toilet and things were falling out of his pockets, but he was squirming and he was a bit on the heavy side, so the two bullies were unable to reach the flush button. So, hearing that someone else was in the bathroom, they called for help.

Mack opened the stall door and immediately saw the problem.

"It's a self-flushing toilet," Mack pointed out.

"Duh, we're not morons," Matthew said.

"Then you actually need to move Horace away from the toilet before the flush will activate," Mack explained.

"That would defeat the entire purpose of a swirlie," Camaro said. Camaro was not stupid; she was just hostile.

"Yeah," Matthew agreed, not sure what he had just agreed to.

"There's a manual override button," Camaro

pointed out, shifting her grip on Horace's ankle.

"Yes," Mack agreed. "But I don't see why I should help you torture Horace."

"Because we'll kick your butt," Matthew said.

This is where a sensible kid would have said, "Good point," and pushed the manual flush button. But Mack had never been accused of being sensible. He had an innate dislike for bullies.

So he said, "You can try."

"Try what?" Matthew asked, baffled.

"He means," Camaro explained patiently, "that we can try to kick his butt. He's implying that we are unable to kick his butt."

Camaro was an attractive girl in a bodybuilder, zero-percent-body-fat, sleek, and predatory sort of way.

"You see," Camaro explained in the pedantic manner that had made her a natural fit for the job of bullying geeks, "he's trying to trick us into putting Horace down and chasing him."

Mack nodded, acknowledging the truth. "You see right through me."

"Mack, Mack, Mack," Camaro said. "You're cute."

"I am," Mack agreed.

"I don't want to beat you up," Camaro admitted. "So why don't you just run away?"

Mack sighed. "Okay. But I'm taking this." He reached down and snagged Matthew's book bag. It was surprisingly light since it contained no books— just a pack of Red Vines licorice, a Mountain Dew, and a pair of nunchakus.

This Matthew understood. He released Horace, which put all the weight on Camaro, who was strong but not that strong. Horace plunged but did not swirl. Matthew leaped, but Mack leaped faster.

Mack was out the door, racing down the hallway with Matthew in lumbering pursuit.

Timing worked in Mack's favor. (He had of course noticed the clock on the wall.) The bell rang, ending the school day, and kids exploded from classrooms like buckshot from a shotgun.

Mack unzipped Matthew's book bag, scattering Red Vines everywhere in the crush of frenzied kids.

Mack had a detailed map of the school in his head. He knew every door, every locker, and every closet. He knew which were unlocked, which exits were alarmed, and where an open window might be found.

He had very little concern that Matthew or Camaro, who had now joined the chase, would actually catch him. He dodged into the chem lab and took the connecting door through to the former chem lab. It was being remodeled following an unfortunate explosion. He noted a ladder, and the roller tray of paint that was perched atop the ladder. He placed Matthew's book bag just so, beneath the ladder.

The windows were open to allow for ventilation, and the painters were on break outside. Mack slid out through the window just as Matthew rushed into the first lab.

Mack crouched outside, just out of sight but not out of hearing, and waited.

"Hey!" Matthew yelled.

Pause.

Mack heard the sound of Matthew's knees popping as he knelt down to pick up his bag.

And then . . . *thunk*! Followed by a soggy clattering sound and a cry of pain.

"Arrggh!" Matthew yelled.

Mack knew he shouldn't risk it but he did

anyway—and peeked. Matthew's head was dripping with pale yellow paint. It ran down his face and into his yelling, aggrieved mouth.

Camaro was a half step behind him.

She spotted Mack and was after him in a heart-beat.

Across the open space between Building A and Building C, Mack found an open door. He ran into a crush of kids very similar to those he'd left behind. He worked his way against the flow, intending to exit by the far door, the one that led to the gym.

But then, to his horror, he saw a massive blond beast just coming in through that very door.

No way he could have known that Stefan Marr would be coming from the gym, having previously forgotten his gym clothes and needing (badly) to take them home to be washed.

"Bluff it through," Mack told himself.

He smiled at Stefan and started to walk very calmly past him. Ten feet and he would be safe. Stefan didn't even know Mack was fleeing.

But then Camaro's voice, a hoarse roar, rose above the happy hubbub. "Bully emergency!" she cried. "I'm declaring a bully emergency!"

Mack's eyes went wide.

Stefan's eyes narrowed.

Mack leaped for the door, but Stefan wasn't one of those great big guys who's kind of slow and awkward. He was one of those great big guys who was as fast as a snake.

One massive paw shot out and grabbed Mack's T-shirt, and suddenly Mack's feet were no longer in contact with the floor.

He did a sort of Wile E. Coyote beat-feet air-run thing, but the effect was more comical than effective.

Camaro and a paint-dripping Matthew were there in a flash.

"Bully emergency?" Stefan asked. "You two can't handle this runt?"

"Look what he did to me!" Matthew cried, outraged.

"You know the rules," Camaro said to Stefan. "We dominate through fear. A threat to one of us is a threat to us all."

Stefan nodded. "Huh," he said. The word *huh* was roughly one-third of Stefan's vocabulary. It could mean many things. But in this case it meant, "Yes, I agree that you have properly invoked a bully emergency, in which all bullies must unite to confront a common threat."

"Better round everyone up," Stefan said. "The usual."

Everyone meant all the other bullies. *The usual* meant the usual place: the Dumpster behind the gym and up against the fence.

"I am going to mess up your face!" Matthew raged at Mack. He pointed for emphasis with a hand dripping pale yellow paint.

"Not the face," Camaro said. "I like his face."

Matthew and Camaro went off in pursuit of the others, while Stefan, seeming more weary than highly motivated, stuffed his sweaty shorts into Mack's mouth and dragged him outside.

This was the point where Mack should have started begging, pleading, whining, and bribing. But the weird thing about Mack was that even though he was afraid of puppets, sharks, the ocean, shots, spiders, dentists, fire, Shetland ponies, hair dryers, asteroids, hot-air balloons, blue cheese, tornadoes, mosquitoes, electrical outlets, bats (the kind that fly and suck your blood), beards, babies, fear itself, and especially being buried alive, he was not afraid of real, actual trouble.

Which, when you think about it, is what tends to get heroes and those around them killed.

Two

A REALLY, REALLY LONG TIME AGO ...

Grimluk was twelve years old. Like most twelve-year-olds he had a job, a child, two wives, and a cow.

No. No, wait, that's not true. He had one wife and two cows.

Grimluk's wife was called Gelidberry. Their baby son's name was as yet undetermined. Picking names was a very big deal in Grimluk's village. There wasn't a lot of entertainment, so when the villagers had something other than eking out a miserable existence to occupy their minds, they didn't rush it.

The cows didn't have names either, at least not that they had shared with Grimluk.

The five of them—Grimluk, Gelidberry, baby, cow, and cow—lived in a small but comfortable home in a village in a clearing surrounded by a forest of very tall trees.

In the clearing the villagers planted chickpeas. Chickpeas are the main ingredient in hummus, but the discovery of hummus would take another thousand years. For now the chickpea farmers planted, watered, and harvested chickpeas. The village diet was 90 percent chickpeas, 8 percent milk—supplied by cow and cow—and 2 percent rat.

Although, truth be told, not a single one of the villagers could have calculated those percentages. Math was not a strong suit of the villagers, who, as well as not being math prodigies, were illiterate.

Grimluk was one of the few men in the village not involved in the chickpea business. Because he was quick and tireless, he had been chosen as the baron's horse leader. This was a very big honor, and the job paid well (one large basket of chickpeas per week, a plump rat, and one pair of sandals each year). Grimluk wasn't rich, but he earned a living; he was doing all right. He couldn't complain.

Until . . .

One day Grimluk was leading his master's horse when he spotted a hurried, harried-looking knave who, judging by the fact that his clothing was colored by *light* brown mud rather than good, honest *dark* brown mud, was not from around these parts.

"Master!" Grimluk said. "A stranger."

The baron—a man with more beard than hair—twisted around as best he could in order to see the stranger in question. It was an awkward thing to do since the baron was facing the horse's tail as he rode. But he managed it without quite falling off.

"I don't know the knave. Ask him his name and business."

Grimluk waited until the stranger was in range, loping and wheezing along the narrow forest trail. Then he said, "Knave? My master would know your name and business."

"My name is Sporda. And my business is fleeing. I'm a full-time fleer. If you have any sense you'll join me in that line of work." He glanced meaningfully back over his shoulder.

"Ask the knave why he is fleeing, and why we should flee," the baron demanded.

The stranger had been brought up well enough to pretend he hadn't heard the baron's question, and waited patiently for Grimluk to repeat it.

Then the stranger said the words that would haunt Grimluk for the rest of his very, very long life. "I flee the . . . the . . . Pale Queen."

The baron jerked in astonishment and slid off the horse. "The . . . ," he said.

"The . . . ," Grimluk repeated.

"The . . . Pale . . . ," the baron said.

"The . . . Pale . . . ," Grimluk repeated.

"No . . . no, it cannot . . ."

"No . . . ," Grimluk said, doing his best to replicate the baron's white-faced horror. "No, it cannot . . ."

The baron could say no more. So Grimluk said no more.

Only Sporda had anything else to say. And what he said then also changed Grimluk's life. "You know, if your master sat facing the other way on that horse, facing the horse's head instead of his tail? He wouldn't need you to guide him."

In less time than it took a rooster to summon the morning sun, Grimluk had lost his job as a horse leader and been forced to switch to a far less lucrative career: fleer.

Three

So, back in the present day, Mack was waiting to get his butt kicked. Stefan kept his iron grip on Mack's shirt and insisted that Mack keep chewing on Stefan's unpleasant gym clothes.

They had reached the usual spot. Big green Dumpster. Chain-link fence. Cinder block back wall of the gym. Asphalt underfoot. No teachers, cops, principals, parents, or superheroes anywhere in sight.

Mack was going to get a beating. Not his first. But

the first since sixth grade. One month into the new school year, and he was already in the grip of Stefan Marr.

"I'm thirsty," Stefan said.

"Mmm hngh nggg uhh hmmmhng," Mack offered.

"Nah, that's okay," Stefan said. "I guess this won't take long."

Sure enough, Matthew and Camaro had been able to quickly assemble the available Richard Gere bullies. Six boys and Camaro were striding toward them with a purposeful, thuggish stride.

Mack had one and only one possible escape route. There was a fire door in the back of the gym. It had frosted reinforced glass that revealed nothing of what was on the other side, but Mack knew the cheerleaders would be practicing just beyond that door.

He also knew the door was supposed to be locked at all times. But Coach Jeter sometimes unlocked it and turned off the alarm so that he could sneak out between classes and smoke a cigarette here in the alley.

Mack had one chance.

He waited, gathered his strength and focus. He

went limp, almost collapsing. And in the split second that Stefan took to adjust his stance, Mack lunged.

His T-shirt ripped away in a single piece, leaving behind only the neck band.

He broke free.

Three steps to reach the door. One, two, three! He snatched at the handle and yanked hard.

The door did not open.

Mack sensed movement behind him.

He spun. Stefan's fist flew and Mack ducked.

Crash!

"Yaaaah!" Stefan cried.

Mack jerked away, off balance, feet tangled. But he didn't fall. He backpedaled, needing just to get his feet back under him.

Then he saw the red spray all over the shattered window.

Stefan's fist had gone through the glass. He had a four-inch gash in his arm, like a red mouth, spurting.

The approaching bullies froze.

Stefan stared in fascinated horror at his arm.

The bullies hesitated, almost decided to keep coming, but then, with a sensible assessment of the risks involved, decided it was time to run away.

They turned tail and bolted, yelling threats over their shoulders.

Stefan used his left hand to try and stop the blood flow.

"Huh," he said.

"Whoa," Mack mumbled with a mouth full of shorts.

"I'm kind of bleeding," Stefan observed. Then he sat down too fast and landed too hard, and Mack realized that what he was seeing here was not a painful but well-timed minor injury. Way too much blood was coming out of Stefan's arm. There was already a puddle of it on the ground—a little pool was forming around a discarded candy bar wrapper.

The king of the bullies tried to stand up, but his body wasn't working too well it seemed, so he stayed down.

Mack stared in amazement. In part he was terrified that he was on the verge of acquiring a whole new phobia: hemaphobia—fear of blood.

Escape would be easy. And Mack definitely considered running.

Instead he spit out the shorts. He straddled the seated Stefan and said, "Lie back."

When Stefan didn't seem to track on that, Mack pushed him none too gently onto his back.

Mack then knelt over Stefan and pushed down with the heel of his left hand on the wound. This was deeply unpleasant. The blood flow slowed but did not stop.

With his free hand Mack grabbed the aromatic T-shirt and clumsily tied it around Stefan's massive bicep. He knotted it tight, all while keeping his palm pressed down on the red gusher.

The blood flow slowed some more.

"I can't keep this up; we need help," Mack said.

Stefan's eyes flickered with what would surely be a temporary understanding of the word *we*.

A powerful word, *we*.

"You have a cell phone?" Mack asked. Cells were absolutely banned at school, so only about two-thirds of the students carried them.

Stefan nodded. His never exactly perky expression was even duller than usual. But he jerked his chin toward his pants pocket.

"Okay, you need to pull on this tourniquet, right?" Mack said. Seeing the blank expression, Mack explained, "The shirt. Pull on the knot with your left hand. Pull hard."

Stefan managed to do this but barely. Mack noticed that his fingers were clumsy, fumbling. His strength was fading.

Mack pried the cell out of Stefan's pants pocket and dialed 911.

"Nine-one-one, what is the nature of your emergency?" a bored voice asked.

"I have a nine-year-old boy pumping blood all over the place," Mack said.

"Nine?" Stefan asked, like he wasn't totally sure it wasn't true.

"They'll come faster for a bleeding kid than a bleeding teenager," Mack explained, covering the mouthpiece. "Now shut up."

It took eight minutes for the ambulance to arrive, which, as it turned out, was barely fast enough.

After the EMTs took Stefan away, Mack made it home unmolested by any more bullies, possibly because he was shirtless except for the neck band of his destroyed T-shirt, and his hands were red with blood up to the elbows. That sort of fashion choice tends to discourage people from bothering you.

Mack's father was home when Mack came in the side door. His father was staring into the refrigerator with the door open, looking like he might see something really cool there if he just kept searching.

"Hey, big guy," his father said.

"Hey, Dad," Mack said.

"How was school?"

"Enh," Mack said. "School's school."

"Yeah. I hear you," Mack's dad said without looking up.

Mack headed toward the stairs and the shower.

Four

Let's just skip the part where Stefan lost two pints of blood. And the part where the doctor told him he could easily have ended up dead.

Let's skip over the slow workings of Stefan's mind as he sought to make some sense of the fact that he had come quite close to dying at the age of fifteen.

And while we're doing that, let's skip over the fact that Mack's father didn't notice that Mack was more or less covered in blood.

Mack's parents didn't pay a lot of attention to him.

It wasn't really sad or tragic. They weren't bad parents. It was just that at some point they had given up trying to figure Mack out.

He'd had one phobia or another since age four. His mother had tried many, many, many (many) times to talk him through these irrational fears. His father had tried as well. And sometimes both at once. And sometimes both at once with a school counselor. And a minister. And a shrink. Two shrinks. Two shrinks, two parents, a minister, a school counselor. But they had never had much success.

In between talking Mack out of being terrified of things that weren't really scary, they had tried to talk him into being scared of things he actually should be afraid of.

Things like bullies, for example.

The boy had no sense. That was clear to his parents and everyone else. The boy simply had no sense.

So, over time, Mack's parents had learned to steer around him. They'd given him his own space. Which was how he liked it. Mostly.

Mack assumed that when Stefan returned to school he would have to demonstrate his toughness by giving Mack a serious beat-down. The upside was that in anticipation of the epic bloodbath, the other bullies were leaving Mack alone. It was just possible that Stefan would be irritated with any bully who presumed to prebeat Mack. No one wanted to deny Stefan his clear rights.

So in the short term, things were good for Mack in the aftermath of the Wednesday Massacre (as it came to be called).

Stefan was not back at school on Thursday or Friday.

"Maybe he croaked after all," Mack said to himself on Friday. "And that would be bad. Yes; bad."

But when Monday rolled around, that guilty hope was banished.

Stefan was definitely not dead. He had a massive bandage on his arm, white gauze wrapped by a sort of weblike thing. But Stefan wouldn't need both arms to murder Mack.

It was a scary moment when Mack looked up and saw Stefan's sullen face at the far end of a hallway full of kids on that fateful Monday.

It was scary for Mack and the few kids who considered him a close friend. But everyone else was just plain giddy. This was the most anticipated moment in the history of Richard Gere Middle School. Imagine the degree of anticipation that might have greeted the simultaneous release of an Iron Man movie, a brand-new sequel to a Harry Potter book, and albums by the top three bands all rolled into one happy, nervous, "OMG, I totally can't wait to see this!" moment.

The kids saw Mack step into the hallway.

They saw Stefan also in the hallway.

The kids parted magically in the middle, as if they were hair and someone had dragged a comb right down the middle of the hallway.

There was a part. That's the point. Kids hugging the lockers to the left. Kids hugging the lockers to the right. And all the kids were incredibly excited.

Mack felt a lump in his throat. He was excited, too, but of course in a very different way. He was excited in the way that had to do with thinking, So, I wonder if there really is an afterlife? That kind of excited.

"Should I run?" Mack wondered.

He sighed. "No. Wouldn't do any good, would it?" No one answered, so he answered himself. "Better to just take my beating here."

If Stefan pounded him here in the hallway, some teacher would probably break it up. Eventually.

So Mack squared his shoulders. He tugged at the back of his T-shirt. He rolled his neck a little, loosening the muscles there. He wasn't going to win this fight, but he was going to try.

Stefan walked straight toward him, his overly adult biceps barely contained by his T-shirt sleeves. Stefan had pecs. Stefan had muscles in his neck. He had muscles in places where all Mack had was soft, yielding flab.

Mack walked toward him and oh, boy, you could have heard a pin drop. So everyone certainly heard it when Santiago dropped his binder and everyone jumped and then giggled—and the anticipation just grew because now it had an element of humor to it.

Stefan came to a stop five feet from Mack.

And at that moment, a very, very old man wearing a black robe that kind of hung down over his face—a man who Mack could not help but notice smelled like some unholy combination of feet, garbage cans, and Salisbury steak—simply appeared.

Appeared as in, "Not there," followed immediately by, "There."

"Ret click-ur!"

That's what the apparition cried. And no, it did not make any sense.

And weirdly all the kids in the hallway—all except for Mack and Stefan—were bathed in a sort of overbright light. It was like the light in a bus station bathroom. Wait, you've probably never been in a bus station bathroom (lucky for you), so imagine the kind of light you'd get if you floated up and stuck your face in a Wal-Mart ceiling light.

It was an eerily bright light of a color that seemed to drain all signs of life out of normal kids' faces.

"Hold!" the old man said in a whiny, hectoring croak of a voice.

And he lifted one wrinkled, age-spotted hand. The fingernails were long and yellow. The cuticles were greenish. Not happy, flowery meadow-green but moldy, eewww-something-is-growing-on-this-sandwich green.

The aromatic, ancient, green-nailed apparition stared at nothing. Not at Mack. Not at Stefan. Possibly because his eyes were like translucent blue marbles. Not blue with a little black dot in the middle and a lot of white all around, but a sort of smeary blue that covered iris, pupil, and all the other eye parts. As if he had started with normal blue eyes, but they'd been pureed in a blender and then poured back into his eyeholes.

Mack froze.

Stefan did not freeze. He frowned at the ancient man and said, "Back off, old dude."

"Touch ye not this Magnifica," the old man said. And he stepped between Stefan and Mack and spread his arms wide.

Then he dropped his arms, seeming too tired to hold them up.

"Fie-ma (sniff) noyz or stib!"

At least that's what Mack thought he said. That's what it sounded like.

And suddenly Stefan was clutching at his chest like something was going very wrong inside. His face began to turn red. He didn't seem to be breathing very well. Or at all.

"Hey!" Mack yelled.

Stefan definitely did not look good.

"Hey, hey, hey!" Mack protested. He had some questions for the old man, starting with, Who are you? Where did you come from? How did you just appear? And even, What's that smell? But none of those was quite as urgent as the question he did ask.

"Hey, what are you doing to him?"

The old man's eyebrows lifted. He turned toward Mack. His creepy blue eyes were on him without seeming to focus, and he said, "He may harm you not."

"That's fine, Yoda, but he's not breathing!"

The old man shrugged. "It matters not. My strength fails."

And sure enough Stefan coughed and then sucked air like a drowning kid who had just barely made it up off the bottom of the pool.

The old man blinked. He seemed perplexed. Lost. Or maybe confused.

"I fade." The old man sighed. His shoulders slumped. "I weaken. I will return when I am able."

Then, with a wheeze, he added, "My head hurts."

And he was gone. As suddenly as he had appeared.

His smell left with him. And the light.

And suddenly, the kids were moving again. Their eyes were bright in anticipation again.

Mack looked at Stefan. "I know you have to beat me up and all," Mack said to Stefan, "but before you do, just tell me: Did you see that?"

"The old guy?"

"So you did," Mack said. "Whoa."

"How did you do that?" Stefan asked.

"I didn't," Mack admitted, although maybe he should have pretended he did.

"Huh," Stefan commented.

"Yeah."

The two of them stood there, considering the flat-out impossible thing that had just happened. Mack could not help but notice that none of the other kids in the hallway seemed upset or weirded out or even curious, aside from a certain curiosity as to why Stefan had not yet killed Mack.

They hadn't seen any of it. Only Mack and Stefan had.

"I wasn't going to kick your butt anyway," Stefan said.

Mack raised one skeptical eyebrow. "Why not?"

"Dude—you saved my life."

"Just now you mean?"

"Whoa!" Stefan said. "That makes two times. You totally saved my life, like . . . twice." He'd had to search for the word *twice*, and he seemed pretty pleased to be able to come up with it.

Mack shrugged. "I couldn't let you bleed to death, or even choke. You're just a bully. It's not like you're evil."

"Huh," Stefan said.

"Kick his butt already!" Matthew shouted. He'd tolerated this cryptic conversation for as long as he could. He had waited patiently for this moment, after all, for the king of all bullies to destroy the boy who had caused him to be painted yellow.

Bits of yellow could still be seen in the creases of Matthew's neck and in his ears.

Stefan processed this for a moment. Then he said words that sent a shock through the entire student body of Richard Gere Middle School. "Yo," he said. "Listen up," he added. "MacAvoy is under my wing."

"No way!" Matthew snarled.

So Stefan took two steps. His face was very close to Matthew's face, and a person who didn't know better might think they were going to kiss.

That was not happening.

Instead, Stefan repeated it slowly, word by word. "Under. My. Wing."

Which settled it.

Five

A REALLY, REALLY LONG TIME AGO . . .

So twelve-year-old Grimluk hit the road as a fleer. He wasn't quite sure why he was supposed to flee from the Pale Queen, but he knew that's what people did. And in those days long, long ago, smart people didn't ask too many questions when they heard trouble was on the way.

Grimluk rounded up Gelidberry, their nameless

baby son, and the cows, and hit the road.

They carried with them all their most prized possessions:

- One thin mattress made of straw and pigeon feathers that was home to approximately eighty thousand bedbugs—although Grimluk could never have conceived of such a vast number
- A lump of clay shaped like a fat woman with a giant mouth that was the family's goddess, Gordia
- One small hatchet with sharpening stone
- A cook pot with an actual metal handle (the family's most valuable object and one of the reasons many others in the village were jealous of Grimluk and thought he and his family were kind of snooty)
- One jar of bold ale, a beverage made of fermented milk and cow sweat flavored with crushed nettles
- The tinderbox, which contained a piece of rock, a sliver of steel that had once chipped off the baron's sword, and a tiny bundle of dry grass

- Gelidberry's sewing kit, consisting of a thorn with a hole in one end, a nice spool of cowtail-hair thread, and a six-inch-square piece of wool
- The family spoon

Other than this they had the clothes on their backs, their foot wrappings, their caps, the baby's blanket, and various lice, fleas, ticks, crusted filth, and face grease.

"I can't believe we've acquired all this stuff," Grimluk complained. "I was hoping to travel light."

"You're a family man," Gelidberry pointed out. "You're not just some carefree nine-year-old. You have responsibilities, you know."

"Oh, I know," Grimluk grumbled. "Believe me, I know."

"Just point the way and let's get going," Gelidberry said, gritting her teeth—she had six, so her gritting was a subtle dig at Grimluk, who had only five.

"The Pale Queen comes from the direction of the setting sun. We'll go the other way."

So off they went toward the rising sun. Which was rather hard to do since in the deep forest one seldom saw the sun.

They walked with the cows and took turns carrying the baby. The mattress was strapped to one of the cows while the other cow carried the pot.

At night they lay the mattress down on pine needles. The three of them squeezed together on it, quite cozy since it was still the warm season.

They rose each day at dawn. They milked the cows and drank the milk. Sometimes Grimluk would manage to hit an opossum or a squirrel with his ax. Then Gelidberry would start a fire, cook the meat in the pot, and they would hand the spoon back and forth.

From time to time they would encounter other fleeing families. The fleers would exchange information on the path of the Pale Queen. It was pretty clear that she was coming. Some of the fleers had run into elements of the Pale Queen's forces. It was easy to spot the people who'd had that kind of bad luck because they didn't always have the full number of arms (two) or legs (also two). Many had livid scars or terrible wounds.

Clearly fleeing was called for. But Grimluk still had no idea what the Pale Queen herself was, or what her agenda might be. None of the others he met had seen her.

Another way of putting it was that those who had seen the Pale Queen were no longer in any position to flee or tell tales.

But it happened that on their fifth night in the forest, Grimluk came to a better understanding of just what or whom he was fleeing.

He was out hunting in the forest, armed with his hatchet. The forest was a frightening place, full as it was of wolves and werewolves, spirits and gnomes, flesh-eating trees and flesh-scratching bushes.

It was dark in the forest. Even in the day it was dark, but at night it was so dark under the high canopy of intertwined branches that Grimluk could not see the hatchet in his own hands. Or his hands, either. Let alone fallen branches, twisted roots, gopher holes, and badly placed rocks.

He tripped fairly often. And there was really very little chance that he would come across an animal to strike with his hatchet. No chance, really. But the baby was teething and therefore crying quite a bit, and Grimluk hated that incessant crying so much that even the forest at night seemed preferable.

As he was feeling his way carefully through the

almost pitch black, he saw light ahead. Not sunlight or anything so bright, just a place where it seemed starlight might reach the forest's floor.

He headed toward that silvery light, thinking, Hey, maybe I'll find an opossum after all. And then I will rub it in Gelidberry's face.

Not the opossum. The fact that he'd found something to eat. That's what he would rub in her face. Because Gelidberry had accused him of only pretending to hunt so that he could get away from the crying, crying, crying.

Grimluk expected to find a clearing. But the trees did not thin out. Instead, he noticed that he was heading downhill. The farther downhill he went, the more light there was. Soon he could see the willow branches that lashed his face and make out some of the larger rocks that bruised his toes.

"What's this about?" Grimluk wondered aloud, reassured by the sound of his own voice.

He heard a sound ahead. He froze. He listened hard and tried to peer through the gloom.

He crept, silent as he could make himself. He crouched and crept and squeezed the handle of the ax for comfort.

He moved closer and closer, as if he could no longer stop himself. As if the light was drawing him forward.

Then . . .

Snap!

The sound came from behind him! Grimluk spun around and stared hard into the utter darkness. It was too late to go back now—something was there.

Grimluk now had an unknown terror behind and a light that seemed ever more eerie ahead. He lay flat and breathed very quietly.

There was definitely something moving behind him and coming closer. Something too large to be a tasty opossum.

Grimluk wished with all his heart that he could be back at the little campsite with the screeching nameless baby and Gelidberry and the cows. What would happen to them if he never returned?

Grimluk crawled on his belly, away from the approaching sound, toward the light, farther and farther down the slope.

And there! Ahead in the clearing . . . a girl!

She was beautiful. Beauty such as Grimluk had never seen or even imagined. Beauty that could not be real.

She was perhaps his age, although there was an age-lessness to her pale, perfect skin. She had wild red hair, long curls that seemed to move of their own accord, twisting and writhing.

Her eyes were green and glowed with an inner light that pierced him to his very soul.

She had a sullen mouth, full red lips, and more teeth than Grimluk and Gelidberry combined. In fact, she seemed, miraculously, to have all of her teeth. And those teeth were white. White without even a touch of yellow.

She wore a dark red dress that lay tight against her body.

Grimluk realized with a shock that the light he had seen was coming from her. Her very skin glowed. Her eyes were green coals. Her hair glistened as it moved.

"Who comes hither?" the girl asked, and Grimluk knew, knew deep down inside, that he would answer, that he would stand up, brush himself off, and answer, "It's me, Grimluk."

But he also knew this would be a bad thing. No creature could possibly be this beautiful, this bright, this clean, this toothy, unless she was a witch. Or some other unnatural creature.

As he was in the act of standing up, a voice spoke from the darkness behind him.

"Your servants, Princess."

The voice was definitely foreign. It wasn't simply that the voice spoke the common tongue with an accent; it was that it seemed to form sounds within that speech that were unlike anything that could come from a human mouth.

A dry, rasping, irritating, whispery voice in response to the cold, confident voice of the stunning object identified as "Princess."

"Ah," the girl said. "At last. You have kept me waiting."

Grimluk heard things moving from behind him, more than one thing—several things, maybe as many as six. Or some other very large number.

He crouched and did not move. If he could have stopped the very beating of his heart, he would have. For the creatures that now emerged into the light of the princess's perfect form were monsters.

They stood as tall as the tallest man (five feet, three inches). But they were not men.

Like huge insects they were, like locusts that walked erect. They moved with sliding steps of bent-back legs and planted clawlike feet. Jointed arms stuck out from the middle of their foul, ochre-tinged bodies. And a second set of arms, smaller than the first, emerged from just below what might be a neck.

And the heads . . . smoothly triangular, with bulging, wet-shining eyes mounted atop short stalks.

They were hideous and awful. And from their midsections—not waists so much as precarious narrowings—hung belts that held varieties of bright metal weapons. Knives, swords, maces, scrapers, darts, and all manner of objects for stabbing, cutting, slicing, dicing, and chopping.

Grimluk hoped they were simply well-equipped cooks, but he doubted it. They moved with an arrogant swagger, not unlike the way the baron moved—or would have, had he been a very large grasshopper.

They gathered around the princess, illuminated by her own light.

For a moment Grimluk feared for the girl. They were a desperate, frightening bunch and looked as if they could make short work of the red-haired beauty.

But the girl showed no fear.

"Faithful Skirrit minions, do you bring me news of the queen, my mother?" she asked.

"We do," one of the bugs answered.

"Good. You have done well to find me. And I will hear all you can tell me, gladly. But first, I hunger."

This news caused a certain shuffling and backpedaling among the Skirrit.

"Hungry?" their spokesman or leader asked with what must be nervousness among his kind. "Now?"

"One will be enough," the princess said.

The Skirrit captain pointed his two left-side arms at one of his fellows. "You heard the princess," he said.

The designated Skirrit drew a deep breath and released a shuddery sigh. Then he bent his long legs and knelt down. He bowed his triangular head, and his ball eyes darkened.

And then the princess, the beauty beyond compare, began to change.

Her body . . . her form . . .

Grimluk had to clap both his hands over his mouth to stop the scream that wanted to tear at his throat.

The princess . . . no, the monstrosity she had

become—the evil, foul beast—opened her stretched and hideous mouth and calmly bit the bowed head from its neck.

Green fluid spurted from the insect's neck. The headless body collapsed with a sound like sticks falling.

And the princess chewed as if she had popped an entire egg into her mouth.

Grimluk ran, ran, ran, tripping and falling and leaping up to run again through the black night.

He ran, shrieking silently in his mind, from the terror.

Six

Mack's parents always asked him about his day at school. But he'd never quite believed they cared about the actual details. At dinner that evening he put his theory to the test.

"So, David, how was school?" his father asked as he tonged chicken strips onto his plate.

His parents called him David. It was his actual name, of course, the name they'd picked out for him when he was just a slimy newborn. So he tolerated it.

"Bunch of interesting stuff happened today," Mack said.

"And don't just tell us it was the same old, same old," his mother said. She passed ketchup to her husband.

"Well, it definitely wasn't the same old, same old," Mack said. "For one thing, some ancient dead-looking dude froze time and space for a while."

"How did the math test go?" his father asked. "I hope you're keeping up."

"That wasn't today. That was Friday. Today was the whole deadish guy suspending the very laws of physics and speaking in some language I didn't understand."

"Well, you've always done well in your language classes," Mack's mother said.

"Plus, it seems I'm Stefan's new BFF."

"A B and two Fs?" His father frowned and shook salt onto mashed potatoes. "That doesn't sound good. You need to crack the books."

Mack stared at his father. Then at his mother. It was one thing to have a theory that they didn't really know him or listen to a word he was saying. It was a very different feeling to prove it.

It made him feel just a little bit lonely, although he wouldn't have wanted to use that word.

After dinner he went to his room and found himself already sitting there.

"Aaaah!" Mack yelled.

"Aaaah!" Mack yelled back.

Mack stood frozen in the doorway, staring at himself sitting on the edge of the bed staring back at Mack in the doorway.

Although, on closer examination, it wasn't him. Not entirely him, anyway. The Mack sitting on the edge of the bed looked a lot like Mack, but there were subtle differences. For one thing, this second Mack had no nostrils.

Mack slid into the room and closed the door behind him.

"All right, who are you?"

"David MacAvoy."

Mack would not have believed that staring at himself could be quite so disturbing. But it was. His mouth had gone dry. His heart was pounding. There seemed to be a ringing sound in his ears, and it was not the sound of happy sleigh bells; it was more like car alarms going off.

"Okay, great trick," Mack said. "I totally see that this is a great trick. I'm not freaking out, I'm laughing at the amazingness of this trick. Ha-ha-ha! See? I'm getting the joke."

"Ha-ha-ha!" the other Mack echoed. And he made a grin with the mouth below the nostril-less nose. The mouth revealed white tooth. Not teeth. Tooth. The entire line of teeth was a curved white solid surface.

The two Macks stared at each other for a while, although Mack Number One did the better job of staring since the other Mack's eyes tended not to point in quite the same direction. The right eye was fine, staring confidently at Mack's face. But the left eye seemed to prefer staring at Mack's knee.

"Okay, this is . . . um . . ." Mack didn't exactly know what it was. So he started over. "Okay, whatever this is, I'd like it to stop now. We both had a good laugh. Whoever you are, kudos. Nicely done. Now take off the mask."

"The mask?"

"The *me* face. Take it off. I want to see who you really are."

"Oh. You want to see my true face?"

"There you go, that's exactly right, dude; I want to see the real you."

The face, the mask—whatever it was—melted.

"Yaaaahhh!" Mack cried, and fumbled behind him for the door handle.

The face that looked very much like his own had grown darker, lumpier, cruder. Dirty. In fact, more than dirty: it was dirt.

Mack was staring at a thing made of mud. Like something a child would make playing in the dirt. Only full-size. And wearing his clothes.

The dirt creature had a mouth but no eyes. No teeth in that mouth, just a horizontal slit.

Mack's fingers were numb on the doorknob. His whole body was tingling from the effect of hormones flooding his system with the urgent desire to *get out*.

But he couldn't turn away. He couldn't stop staring at the mud face and the mud hands. There even seemed to be bits of gravel and small twigs in that mud face.

When the thing opened its mouth, Mack swore he saw a piece of paper, maybe the size of a Post-it, but curled up in a tube.

"Okay. Let's try the other face again," Mack whispered.

Slowly the mud grew pink. The slit of a mouth formed lips. Eyes like mucous globules formed in the right places and slowly acquired semihuman characteristics. Hair sprouted, looking at first like an eruption of earthworms before it settled down and became hair.

Mack whistled softly. There was no doubt in his mind that this, this, this . . . *thing* . . . was related to the ancient man with the ancient smell.

"I've finally gone crazy, haven't I?" Mack said. "I guess it was just a matter of time."

He had the absurd thought at that moment that he still had homework to do. It was right there on his desk.

"Dude. Or whatever you are . . . actually, what are you? Let's start with that."

"I am a golem."

"Gollum?"

"Golem."

"Okay. How do you spell that?"

The golem raised its eyebrows, which kind of stretched its eyelids upward, revealing more eyeball than was right. "G-O-L-E-M."

Mack sidled past the creature and slid into his desk chair. He opened his laptop and clicked on the browser icon.

He typed the word *golem* into the Google search box. The first hit was Wikipedia.

Mack scanned down the page.

"You're Jewish?" he asked the golem.

"I'm whatever you are," the golem answered.

"But golems, they're a Hebrew thing, originally. An incomplete being made of clay."

Mack was just beginning to get the idea that having a golem could be useful. He hadn't quite worked out how, but he was sensing an opportunity there.

"Do you have superpowers?"

The golem shrugged. "I am made to be you."

Mack pushed back from the computer, swiveled his desk chair, and leaned forward with his elbows on his knees.

"Why are you here?"

"I am here to replace you."

That didn't sound good. "Um . . . what?"

"While you are away, I will take your place here."

"Am I going somewhere?"

The golem smiled, revealing its creepy tooth thing and a hint of the little paper scroll. "You are going everywhere."

Seven

The golem was supposed to spend the night on the floor beside Mack's bed. Mack had sneaked an extra blanket and one sheet from the linen closet in the hallway. But when Mack woke up the next morning, he was looking at the golem.

It took him a few seconds to become oriented. He swatted the sheets beside him to ensure that he was in fact lying on his back—that he was faceup, and that his eyes were pointed in that same direction.

The golem was awake, too.

"Dude. Golem. Why are you on the ceiling?"

The golem was apparently quite at ease on the ceiling. He was lying on his back, mirroring Mack. But not quite directly above because there was a ceiling fan in the way.

"Should I come down?"

"I kind of think so."

The golem did not float down or drop down. It stood up, which brought its head down to just a foot above Mack's face. Then it walked to the corner of the room and stepped from the ceiling onto the wall, where it was once again upright. In a horizontal sort of way.

It sidestepped the dresser and stepped from wall to floor.

"I thought you didn't have any superpowers," Mack said.

The golem shrugged. "I am a golem."

"What are we going to do with you, man?" Mack wondered aloud. "I have to go to school. I keep expecting smelly old guy to show up and explain what's going on."

"Smelly old guy?"

"Is he the one who made you? This really old guy with, like, green fingernails?"

"I was made by great Grimluk."

"Grim Look?"

"Grimluk."

"Sometimes the name just fits, you know?"

"Not really."

Mack sighed. He was trying to be a good sport. He was playing along. Mostly because he found golems more interesting than his usual life.

It wasn't that Mack was unhappy. He had nothing to be unhappy about, really. He did okay in school. He had one or two friends, although he didn't think of them as particularly close. But they would say, "Hey, Mack," when he walked by. And sometimes they'd hang out together on a Saturday and maybe even play some ball.

He had parents who weren't mean, kids who kind of liked him, teachers who weren't terrible, a nice house, a nice room, a decent laptop—what was there not to like?

But exciting? As exciting as having time frozen

by ancient apparitions? As exciting as a mythical clay creature who slept on the ceiling?

However, as much as Mack was willing to play along for the sheer adventure of it, he was feeling a need for answers. Question number one: Is this real, or am I having some kind of cosmic kernel panic? Is this the real-life equivalent of the Blue Screen of Death? Did I miss an important software update?

If so, is there some way I can reboot?

Ah, but Mack admitted to himself, you wouldn't reboot this even if you could.

He wasn't looking for a quick, reassuring return to normal. He was anxious for the craziness to move to the next phase.

He noticed the clock.

"I'm late," he said. "Look, Golem, stay clear of my mom, okay? Hide in the closet. Yeah. That's what you do."

"Okay," the golem said.

Mack headed downstairs.

"Make yourself a Breakfast Pocket," Mack's mother said. She was adding creamer to her coffee. The small kitchen TV was on to the news.

"I want a Toaster Strudel," Mack said.

"Breakfast Pocket."

"Okay," Mack said, surrendering. He pulled a Toaster Strudel from the freezer and popped it into the toaster. His mother had never yet noticed that he ignored her on this. Sometimes it puzzled Mack. Didn't she notice when she went to the grocery store that she kept buying Toaster Strudels?

"Have a good day at school," his mother said. She headed toward the garage. "Love you."

"Love you," he called back.

His father was already gone. He had a longer commute.

Mack headed down the street toward his bus stop as his mother backed her car out of the garage.

It was a nice day out, a wide blue sky overhead with just a scattering of cirrus clouds off to the south. The heat of summer was mostly a memory now, and the desert air had just a slight snap to it in the morning. It felt good in Mack's lungs as he trudged down the street to the corner.

Out of the corner of his eye he happened to see an old man coming down the street.

The man was very old and dressed spectacularly, all in shades of green. He was dressed nicely, not like a crazy street person. He wore dark green slacks and a grass-green blazer over a brownish green vest. His shirt was white and starched, the only touch of nongreen aside from brown shoes.

The thing that made the whole outfit kind of work was the green derby hat.

The man in green had a walking stick in one hand and a bulky leather overnight bag in the other. Mack glanced back at him a couple of times but didn't want to look as if he was staring.

Mack spotted the knot of kids waiting for the bus just a few feet ahead: Ellen and Karl from his grade, some younger kids, and one older kid named Gene or John or something.

Mack did the nod-of-acknowledgment thing and got the same in return from Karl.

"Tsup?"

"Enh."

"Tsup?"

"You know."

Mack saw the bus coming down the side street.

It would be here in three minutes. He had timed it before.

Something was wrong. Mack felt it before he knew what it was. But it took only a few seconds to decide what the problem was: the old man in green. He'd been walking this direction. He should still be in view.

But he wasn't. Which meant he had turned off at one of four possible homes on this side of the street. The Reynoldses never answered their door, no matter what; the Applegates were out of town; the Tegens were already at work, and their daughter was standing right here at the bus stop.

Which left the MacAvoy household.

The old man in green was not a yard worker or a plumber or a carpenter or anyone else of the workman breed. So what was he doing? Where did he go?

Mack wanted to go back to check. If he did, he would miss the bus. If he missed the bus, he would miss the bell, even if he ran all the way to school.

That would mean walking into homeroom late. People would stare at him and laugh, and it would be marked on his attendance record.

But he had no choice. His curiosity was piqued,

and he had to go see.

"I forgot something," he said to the other kids, none of whom cared. He began trotting back down the street.

He glanced at the Reynoldses' home. Nothing. The Applegates' home. Nothing. Likewise the Tegens'.

He reached his own home. No green man.

Mack frowned. So he'd been wrong. But then he noticed the fact that the gate to the backyard was slightly ajar. With his heart in his throat, he pushed through the gate.

There was nothing unusual in the yard: the same unused swing set, a basketball rocking slightly in the breeze. Except that there was no breeze.

His father's grill was close at hand. He reached up under the plastic cover, felt around for a moment, and pulled out the big long barbecue fork.

Armed and dangerous with his fork, Mack proceeded.

The back door was shut. But there! The window. The kitchen window. Had it been open before? No. No, he didn't think so. But now it was clearly open a crack.

Mack debated for a second. No way the green man could have slid through the window.

He pulled out his key and unlocked the back door.

"Anybody home?"

No answer.

He considered swapping the fork for a kitchen knife but decided the fork had the added advantage of being so weird no burglar would know quite how to react.

He passed through the kitchen. Now he heard the sound of the TV in the family room. It wasn't loud, and it sounded like a commercial was playing.

Closer and closer Mack crept.

Someone was sitting on the couch, its back turned to Mack.

"Golem?" he called.

The golem stood up and turned, grinning his creepy, not-quite-Mack-like grin.

Mack screamed. Screamed like a little girl.

Attached to the golem's arms, thighs, ankles, belly, and neck were a dozen brown snakes. Each was maybe three feet long, maybe four. Mack wasn't going to measure them.

"Aaaahhhh!" Mack yelled.

The golem hesitated. Then he yelled, too, in a pretty close approximation of Mack's own voice.

"Snakes!" Mack yelled.

"Snakes!" the golem repeated.

"W-w-w-w-why?" Mack stammered.

The golem looked down at the snakes. He plucked the one from his neck and held it out to see it better. The snake hissed and writhed and twisted to sink its fangs into the golem's wrist.

"The man put them in the window," the golem said. "I don't know why."

Mack had not previously suffered from ophidiophobia, although he was pretty sure he would start soon enough.

As mentioned earlier, Mack noticed things. And he remembered the things he had noticed, even when those things involved class field trips to the zoo.

"That's an Australian brown snake, dude!" Mack said.

"Yes, of course, the zoo trip," the golem said.

Mack felt his insides churning. "It's one of the most poisonous snakes on earth."

"Yes, yes, it is," the golem said, and nodded, pleased to have accessed Mack's memories of this normally useless fact. "It doesn't seem to be bothering me."

One of the snakes was eyeballing Mack. Fangs buried in the golem's arm, it was looking straight at Mack. It was not a pleasant look.

He had to get rid of them. It was going to be tough explaining a dozen poisonous vipers to his parents. He and the golem had to get them. Get them all. But how?

"Walk to the kitchen," Mack said.

The golem did.

The snakes were like weird hair extensions hanging from odd parts of him.

"Okay, this is going to be gross," Mack warned.

He threw the switch for the garbage disposal.

The golem detached the first snake and tried to urge it into the roaring hole.

Mack took his barbecue fork and, with extraordinary care and much flinching, pushed the snake in.

Grrrchunkchunkwgheee!

The snakes were not geniuses, that much was clear. They didn't seem to have the sense to let go of the golem and run for it. A second snake followed the first.

Grrrchunkchunkwgheee!

As he murdered snakes, Mack replayed the morning's events in his mind. The man in green had known where he was going. The man in green had never made eye contact with Mack, and at that distance he would surely not have recognized Mack even if he had spotted him.

Everyone knew golems were made of mud. And no one was dumb enough to think that viper poison would kill a golem.

Therefore: the man in green had been trying to kill Mack.

He had actually been trying to *kill* him.

Knowing this made the disgusting sound of the snakes going *grrrchunkchunkwgheee* in the disposal almost musical.

Eight

A REALLY, REALLY LONG TIME AGO . . .

After his run-in with the Skirrit and the princess, Grimluk devoted himself with even more enthusiasm to the job of fleeing.

Fleeing 2.0. A whole new level of fleeing.

He pushed Gelidberry, the cows, and the baby at top speed: three miles an hour.

They fled all through the rest of that first night

and all through the next day. Exhausted and cranky, they arrived toward dusk at the edge of the forest. Ahead of them was a vast open meadow. From the center of the meadow there rose a steep hill. The hill looked as if it had been built entirely of tall, jagged slabs of granite, then decorated with earth and grass and even the occasional tree. And then as if, over many years, most of that blanket of earth had been worn down by rain and snow and whatever mysterious force pulled things down toward the ground (gravity, but that hadn't been discovered yet).

Atop this grim and stony hill sat a castle that looked almost to be carved out of the very stone of the hill. The walls were a dark gray, upswept to crazy heights and then crenellated.

Crenellations: the little jigsaw-looking things at the top of castle walls.

Grimluk hadn't seen that many castles. In fact he'd seen just one, the baron's castle, which, to tell the truth, was about as impressive as an Office Depot.

This castle, on the other hand, had a seriously dangerous look and feel. And even from far off Grimluk could tell that it was on a high state of alert. Spear tips glinted from the crenellations, sunset painting the bronze points red. There were even archers armed with state-of-the-art bows.

The castle was expecting trouble.

Towering above the walls was the keep. The keep was the last resort, a castle-within-a-castle. If enemies breached the outer walls, they then had to start all over again to take the keep.

From the top of the keep fluttered a black and sky-blue banner. There was some sort of symbol on the banner, but Grimluk couldn't quite make it out.

Far below, crouching by the foot of the hill, was a village, a few dozen thatch-roofed buildings.

"Let's go to the village," Grimluk said. "Maybe we can sell some milk and get a room for the night."

"We don't have reservations," Gelidberry pointed out.

But Grimluk didn't care because reservations hadn't yet been invented, let alone Priceline and Expedia and hotels.com. In fact, if there had been any such thing, it would have been called inns.com or even stables.com.

They reached the edge of the village just as night fell. They parked the cows and carried the nameless baby into the first inn they found.

It was crowded with drunken men and a few drunken women. But it was quiet for a room full of drunks. People were more sullen than rowdy. When Grimluk and Gelidberry came in, every eye turned toward them, appraising the tired family.

"How many in your party?" the innkeeper asked.

"Two adults, one child," Grimluk answered.

"We don't have a kids' menu," the innkeeper warned.

They elbowed their way to the end of one of the long tables. Grimluk ordered a tankard of mead and three bowls of gruel. It was a Tuesday: gruel night. Grimluk felt a little disappointed. If he'd come on Monday, it would have been fish and chips.

Across the table sat a burly, older man of perhaps sixteen years. He had a full beard studded with bits of food. Little pig eyes stared out from beneath a scarred, tanned brow. The man had an ax slung over one shoulder. Grimluk fingered his own hatchet and winced to realize that the ax was maybe three times bigger.

"Hi," Grimluk said. "How's the gruel here?"

The man made a deep, grumbly sound that might

have been a sort of restaurant review. Then he said, "You're a stranger, as am I. Do you come to join up?"

"Join up?"

"The Army of Light," the man said. "They're hiring. If you have the right stuff."

"We have two cows," Grimluk said. "And this spoon." He showed the spoon.

The man laughed, a sound that seemed totally out of place in a room where people were mostly whispering and glancing nervously over their shoulders.

"We have no need of spoons! Spoons will not defeat the Pale Queen!"

The whispering came to a very sudden stop. The man winced, clearly embarrassed, as if he'd farted or used an offensive word. (*Soap* was one such offensive word.)

"Sorry. I meant to say, 'the Dread Foe.'"

The people in the room went back to their slurred whispers.

"This Army of Light," Gelidberry said, "do they pay well?"

"Hey, I'm not looking for a job," Grimluk protested.

"You have a family to feed," Gelidberry snapped. "And in case you haven't noticed, you're not doing very well at that." She pointed at her ribs. "I can count these clear through my clothing."

"All right, all right," Grimluk said. He pointedly turned back to the man, ignoring Gelidberry's reproachful gaze. "I used to be horse leader to the baron. Now I'm a fleer."

"Everyone's a fleer nowadays," the man snorted. Then he held out a fat-fingered hand. Grimluk shook it.

"My name is Grimluk."

"Wick," the man said. "I came to join the Army of Light as a pikeman. I could get you in to see the pike captain."

"I have no experience with a pike."

Wick shrugged. "Eh. There's not much to it. It's a big, long spear. You hold the pointy end toward the enemy. I'm not saying there's not some skill involved, but you seem sharp enough."

It took Grimluk a few seconds to think about that. "Sharp enough? Was that a pun?"

Wick chewed at his lip. "I'm not sure. All I know is, they're hiring pikemen. It pays two loaves of bread and a small hatful of cheese curds per week, and they supply the pike."

"I used to earn a large basket of chickpeas and a plump rat per week, and one pair of sandals a year," Grimluk said.

Wick guffawed. "Ha! You won't find that kind of riches carrying a pike, that's for sure. A plump rat? A pair of sandals? That's Magnifica money."

"Magnifica?"

The use of that word had the opposite effect on the room from what the words *Pale Queen* had caused. Instead of stunned silence and fearful glances, Grimluk saw drunken eyes open wide and fill with tears of hope.

"He can do that," Gelidberry said quickly.

Wick shook his head sadly. "Oh, my lady, your confidence does your husband proud, but to be a Magnifica, a man must be no more than twelve years of age."

"He's twelve," Gelidberry said.

"And he must possess the *enlightened puissance*."

That shut Gelidberry up pretty effectively. Because she had no idea what *enlightened puissance* might be.

But by this point Grimluk was feeling a little disrespected, both by Gelidberry and by Wick's casual dismissal of the idea that he might possess *puissance*.

Grimluk had no more idea that Gelidberry had what *enlightened puissance* might be. But he didn't see why he couldn't possess it. Lots of it.

By this point Grimluk had swallowed half the tankard of mead.

"I have that," Grimluk asserted. "I have a bunch of it."

"Of what?" Wick asked cagily, narrowing one narrow eye still further.

"Enlabored pittance," Grimluk said.

"Is that how you pronounce it?" Wick asked.

"In my country, yes," Grimluk said quickly.

"Then you must go. Go! Run to the castle and announce yourself, young man, for they await with ever-growing despair for the twelfth of the twelve!"

"Okay." Then, "What's twelve?"

"Don't be embarrassed," Wick said kindly. "I only learned the concept yesterday myself. Here's what it is: picture eleven. Right? Do you have eleven firmly fixed in your imagination?"

"Yes," Grimluk said doubtfully.

"Well, twelve is one more than eleven."

"What will they think of next?" Gelidberry said.

"Haste! Haste if ye truly possess the *enlightened puissance*." Wick leaned across the table, blasting them with the smells of stale mead, gruel, sweat, horse, goat, leather, very dirty wool, and stable sweepings. "Haste! For surely if we find not the twelfth of the twelve, the Pale Queen . . . I mean . . . the Dread Foe will have us all, pikes or no pikes!"

This put Grimluk in a rather embarrassing situation. He'd opened his big mouth and announced that he had something he'd never seen and wouldn't recognize if he tripped over it. And every tear-brimmed eye gazed at him now with hope and anticipation.

Gelidberry shrugged. "Go. What's the worst that can happen? They'll say no, and you take the pike job."

What neither she, nor Grimluk could possibly know, was that Grimluk did indeed possess the *enlightened puissance*. He had it in spades.

And because he had it, he would never grow old with Gelidberry, or watch the nameless baby grow up.

Nine

Mack was somewhat disturbed by the incident of the snakes. If by "somewhat disturbed," you mean "on the edge of complete meltdown panic."

"That old dude in green was trying to kill me!" Mack wailed as the last of the snakes went noisily down the disposal.

"Yes. I believe he was," the golem agreed.

"Why would he be trying to kill me? I just got

Stefan and the bullies off my back, and now some guy who looks like he came straight from a Saint Patrick's Day parade is trying to viper me to death?"

"I don't understand any of that," the golem said.

Mack grabbed the golem's arm and stared hard into the face that was just like his own. "You need to tell me whatever you know."

The golem shrugged. "I was made to replace you."

"And I need replacing why, again?"

"Because you are leaving."

"And where am I going?"

"Everywhere."

"Aaaarrrgghhh!" Mack yelled in frustration. He had missed his bus. He needed to get to school. He needed to figure out what to do with Clay Boy. He needed to avoid getting bitten to death by snakes. And he was wishing he'd had the Breakfast Pocket because the Toaster Strudel hadn't really filled him up.

"Okay, look," Mack said. "I have to go. You stay away from my folks. Go sit in my room. Do not talk to anyone or answer the door. Will you do exactly what I've just told you?"

"Would you do what you were told?"

Mack's expression darkened. "Oh, it's like that, is it?"

"I am made in your image," the golem pointed out.

Feeling far less than happy, Mack left and headed for school. He slipped in unnoticed just as the bell rang and kids came pouring out of their homerooms on their way to the next stop on the day-long March of Boredom.

"Yo," Stefan said.

Mack was still not used to the idea that he was now under Stefan's wing. His first gut reaction was to run. But that would probably have hurt Stefan's feelings.

"Hey, Stefan," Mack said.

"Where you going?"

"Math."

"Cool. Let's roll."

Mack frowned. "You're not in my math class, Stefan."

"I am now."

"But . . . can you do that?"

"Yes," Stefan said with absolute confidence. And Mack could see his point. Whatever class he was skipping out on, the teacher would be glad to see him go, while the math teacher was not likely to pick a fight with Stefan.

"Fair enough," Mack said. "I have to take a leak first."

"Boys' room? Or you want to use the teachers' lounge?"

"The regular boys' room will be fine," Mack said, although he was beginning to see that there might be some definite advantages to this new relationship with Stefan.

They went to the boys' room, which was moderately full of kids.

"Empty," Stefan said to them, and jerked his chin toward the door.

There was the sound of zippers hastily drawn up and water flushing. In twenty seconds Mack had the boys' room to himself.

"You don't have to do that," Mack said. But the truth was, he kind of enjoyed it. He disliked doing his business in crowds.

Then the light in the boys' room changed.

"What's happening?"

Stefan shrugged. "Light got weird. Like the other day, kinda."

"Uh-oh," Mack said.

The new light seemed to have a more specific source this time. In fact, it came from the shiny chrome pipe above the urinal.

There was a face in the pipe. The face of the old, old man with the bad smell. It was hard to tell whether he had brought his bad smell with him since this was, after all, the boys' room and had its own distinctive aromas.

"You!" Mack said, accusing.

"Can you see me?" the ancient man asked.

"Yes, I can see you. Stefan, can you see him?"

Stefan looked over Mack's shoulder and nodded. He seemed amazingly calm, as if this kind of thing happened all the time. "You want me to smash it?"

"No," Mack said.

"Have you seen the golem?" the ancient creature asked in his dry-leaves voice.

"Yeah. And the snakes," Mack snapped.

"I know not of snakes."

"Yeah, well, I know of them," Mack shot back.

"Some old dude in green stuck 'em in my window. They bit all over the golem."

The ancient's eyebrows shot up. The effect was particularly odd since the round chrome surface exaggerated every expression. "This is very bad news."

"Yeah, I thought so, too," Mack said.

"The forces of the Dread Foe are already aware of you."

"Okay. I don't have any dread foes," Mack said.

"He's under my wing," Stefan added belligerently.

"You have foes of which you dream not," the old man rasped. "Foes which, if you only knew of them, your blood would freeze like a mountain stream in winter and your hands would tremble and lose their strength."

Mack found this alarming. "Hey! I don't have any enemies. I'm not looking for trouble. I have a math test."

"We choose not our enemies. Your foes are the foes of your blood. For in your veins runs the blood true of the Magnifica."

"Is that Latin?"

"You are called, young hero. Called! To save the

world from the nameless evil."

"What's the name of this nameless evil?" Mack asked.

"The Pale Queen! But we name her not."

"You just did."

The old man looked irritated at being caught in a contradiction. "I am trying to move things along. I don't have a lot of time. My magic is weak, nowhere near what it once was. I fail . . . I weaken . . . I can scarce hear you or make myself heard in return."

"Then spit it out, grandpa," Stefan snarled.

The ancient glanced at Stefan. "This one will be useful. You will have need for a wild dog such as this."

Mack thought Stefan might take offense at this, but Stefan only swelled a little bit and nodded in agreement.

"I will spit it," the ancient said. "I am called Grimluk. One of the first great band of heroes called the Magnifica. We it was who first fought the Pale Que—the Dread Foe and bound her tightly within the bowels of the earth never again to trouble poor frightened humanity. We placed spells that would keep the world safe forever!"

"Okay, then we have nothing to worry about, right?" Mack said hopefully.

"Well . . . ," Grimluk said.

"Uh-oh."

"You must understand that this all happened a very long time ago. These were the days before most people knew anything of numbers. We had no algebra. Nor did we partake of geometry. Or long division. Or multiplication."

"So you had . . ."

"We could add and subtract. In theory. In practice most people could count only to ten. Nine if they'd had an accident with a scythe. Which was very common."

"And?" Mack urged.

"And in those long-ago days ten was a very big number. A rich man was an elevenaire. Peasants would fantasize about striking it rich in the lottery and having ten of . . . of anything."

"I would have been happy then," Stefan said thoughtfully.

"So, when we were deciding how long to imprison the Dread Foe, we called upon our greatest astrologers, our mathematical prodigies, importing great thinkers from the four corners of the earth. They worked for weeks and weeks. Maybe as many as eleven weeks to conceive of a number so impossibly large that it would be the greatest number ever conceived by human minds!" He sighed, and for a moment the image faded.

"Hey!"

"Sorry." The face was back. "The number these geniuses conceived was . . . three thousand!"

"So you tied up this Pale Queen for three thousand years."

"Exactly. Forever. Or so we thought. It turns out three thousand years is still not forever. And now the three thousand years has all but run its course. In just a few months the Dread Foe will be loosed in all her fury, all her rage, all her sphincter-clenching, heart-clutching, throat-gobbling, spit-drying, blood-freezing, bowel-loosening terror!"

"Dude. No offense, but you guys had what? Swords? Sticks? Pitchforks? We have guns and tanks and jets. So if this Pale Queen pops up, the marines will take care of her."

"Arrogant young fool!" Grimluk cried, suddenly agitated. "Do you think the Pale Queen slept these long years? Think you that she has no knowledge of your world and its marvels? Ha! All that you possess, she possesses as well. Your knowledge is hers, too. Plus, all the terrible powers of her magic. Your guns will turn to twigs, your deadly craft all obliterated! She comes to kill all she wishes and enslave the rest."

"I don't believe in magic," Mack said.

"Oh? Then how is it that you converse with an image in a mirror?"

Grimluk had him there. Plus there was the golem.

Mack decided against pointing out that it wasn't so much a mirror as a shiny toilet pipe.

"My time is short, Mack of the Magnifica, in whose veins flows the long-attenuated blood of ancient heroes. You must go. Now! For the enemy has your scent, and although the Dread Foe is still bound within her subterranean lair, her minions run riot. The Skirrit, the giant Gudridan, the treasonous Tong Elves, the Bowands, and her own spawn, the Weramin! And forget not her worldly allies, the devious Nafia. It was surely they who attempted to kill you with snakes."

"Okay, enough, all right?" Mack said. It was getting to him. He was feeling fear, true fear, begin to form like a ball in his chest.

"Listen, for my time is run out," Grimluk said. "I will help when I may. You must assemble a new twelve of twelves. Bring the twelve new Magnifica together from the corners of the earth and find a way to bind the Dread Foe again."

"How am I supposed to do this?" Mack demanded. "I'm missing a math test. I have PE next after that. I'm kind of busy."

"Find the way of Vargran, young one. Or truly, all the world will die. But first, if you return to your home and hearth, you will draw the enemy like nectar draws the bee, and all those who know you, all who love you, will be destroyed!"

"Vargran?"

"I fade . . . ," Grimluk said sadly. "Much is left to tell but . . . power . . . no longer . . ." He was flickering now, and the sound of his voice was like a cell phone call breaking up. "You will be . . . contacted."

Then he and his weird light were gone.

"Huh," Stefan said.

"This is nuts," Mack said. "No way. I mean, seriously, someone slipped some bad peanut butter into our cookies or whatever. We're hallucinating."

The bathroom door opened then.

Framed there was the old man in green.

He grinned with surprisingly white teeth. He hefted his walking stick in one hand. He grabbed the knob atop his stick with the other.

And he drew out a very bright, very sharp-looking sword.

Ten

"Have at you!" the green man said.

He lunged at Mack, needle-sharp point thrusting straight toward Mack's heart.

But the man in green was very old. Very old. Probably not as old as the spectral Grimluk, but way old.

So the sword point didn't exactly slice through the air. It was more a case of it trembling forward. Mack leaped to one side, and between the time when he leaped aside and the sword reached the place he'd been, he had time to stop and tie his shoe. Understand—he didn't stop to tie his shoe. But he could have.

The man in green frowned. He stared at the place where Mack had been.

He turned rheumy green eyes left and right and finally located Mack, shrinking up against a stall door.

He began to swing the sword in an arc that would slice Mack right across the throat, if he stood there long enough.

Stefan stepped forward and grabbed the man's sword arm. "Hey. Stop that, old man." He took the sword and the walking stick and thrust the sword back into it. "Cool stick," Stefan observed.

"Unhand me!" the old guy yelled.

"Whatever," Stefan said, and released the man.

"Why are you trying to skewer me?" Mack demanded, outraged.

The old man started to answer, but then raised one finger indicating he needed a moment. He fumbled inside his green blazer and drew out a clear plastic tube that ended in a clear plastic mouthpiece.

He pressed the mouthpiece against his lips and nose and breathed deeply. Once. Twice. Three times. Four times. Five times.

Six times.

And . . . seven.

"Oxygen. I can't take this altitude," he explained.

"Should I call a doctor?" Mack asked.

"Ha!" the man said. "I'll see you in your unmarked grave, you young . . ." He held up his finger again and took several more draws of the oxygen.

"You'll rue the day you ever heard the name Paddy 'Nine Iron' Trout."

"Actually, this is the first I've heard it," Mack pointed out. "And that thing with the snakes was seriously uncool."

"Snakes?" Stefan asked.

"This old dude put poisonous snakes in my window. They would have killed me, too, only they went for the golem."

Stefan nodded as if he understood. He didn't.

"You can run, but you cannot hide from the fist of the Nafia," Nine Iron said. He made a fierce face, and Mack could kind of see where back in the day—like sixty, seventy years ago—it would have been a scary look. Now he mostly noticed the way Nine Iron paused between each word to either lick his lips or suck on his oxygen.

"The Mafia?" Mack asked. "Like Tony Soprano?"

"That was a great show," Stefan said. "Like when Ton' took out Christopha? Cold, man."

"Not the Mafia, the *Nafia*," Nine Iron said. And some time later he waved a dismissive hand. "The Mafia, ha! They got it all from us. Bunch of copycats. Why, when I was a whelp just coming up—"

The story was interrupted by a kid coming in. Stefan jerked his chin at the boy, and they were alone again.

"Okay, look, I have classes to get to," Mack said. "But you have to stop bothering me. I'm not looking for trouble."

"Well, trouble has found you," Nine Iron said. "You think the Great Queen is blind and senile? That old fool Grimluk has put the queen's mark on you, young meddler."

"Queen's mark?"

"You and all those who would help you carry the

mark upon them. All who worship the Pale One will pursue you unto death! Until you and all you love are dead! Dead!" He held up both shaky hands and lifted his watery eyes to the bathroom ceiling. "She comes, bringing everlasting youth and great power to all those who serve her! And for you?" His ancient, wrinkled face was suddenly hard, and his eyes, despite their unfocused yellow look, were lit from within by a hard glint of hatred.

"You"—he pointed his arthritic claw at Mack— "you shall suffer and die! And I will laugh!"

He then laughed, but Mack decided pretty quickly that Nine Iron's prediction wasn't really funny.

"Let's get out of here," Mack said.

"Look you, boy," Nine Iron said, and his voice had grown silky smooth. "I'll make it quick and painless for you. Better to let me do it now than to see your family go first, and you only at the end, and painfully. More painfully than you can possibly imagine."

Mack and Stefan left the old man in the boys' bathroom. A line had formed outside. "Go somewhere else," Stefan said.

Mack walked quickly down the hall. Stefan fell in beside him.

"Where are you going?"

"I don't know," Mack said. "But you heard the guy. Anyone around me could be in trouble."

"You got no worries," Stefan said. "You are under my wing."

"Dude. I seriously appreciate that. But you didn't spend part of your morning grinding up poisonous snakes in a garbage disposal."

"You scared of that old guy? Paddy Wacky, whatever his name was?"

"Yeah," Mack said. "Maybe it's just me, but I start getting kind of nervous when people violate the laws of physics, talking out of toilets and all. Not to mention the whole boy-made-out-of-clay thing. Call me a wuss, but my weird limit has been reached."

"Who's made out of clay?"

"The golem," Mack said. "It's like a medieval creature, a sort of robot made out of clay. I have one."

Stefan nodded thoughtfully. "If I had a robot, I wouldn't want him to be mid-evil. I'd want one that was, like, high-evil."

Mack decided against trying to explain further.

"Where are you going to go?" Stefan asked.

Mack turned and walked backward, holding his hands out in a helpless gesture. "I guess I'm going to go save the world."

"Yeah?" Stefan said. "Okay, then; I'll go, too."

The assistant principal stepped out of his office as they passed. "Just where do you think you're going, Mr. MacAvoy?"

"Saving the world, sir."

They burst through the doors outside. Waiting in the driveway, where parents in minivans would later in the day be lining up to pick up their kids, sat a very long black limousine.

Mack and Stefan came to a stop.

The rear window lowered. Inside sat a woman.

She did not appear to be armed. In fact, she was quite beautiful. Asian, Mack noticed, hair perfect, makeup perfect. Probably not dangerous. But by the same token, probably not there to pick up her kids.

"Come," the woman said.

"Yeah, I don't think so," Mack said, backing away. "I'm not supposed to take rides with strangers. And if there was ever a day for me to listen to that warning, this is it."

"I think you may change your mind," the woman said.

"Nah. Not today. Ma'am."

"Look behind you," the woman said.

Mack did. So did Stefan, who said, "Whoa."

Running with strange, bounding leaps, impossibly fast, impossibly impossible, were two very large grasshoppers standing upright and carrying wicked-looking battle-axes in their middle pair of legs.

"Aaaahhh!" Mack yelled.

"Whoa," Stefan agreed.

Both decided they would enjoy a ride in a limo. They snatched open the door and leaped, practically flying over the woman to land in a confused heap on the carpeted floor.

The door slammed. The window rose. The engine gunned.

One of the big insects was all over the car. It smashed its ax down on the hood. The car kept going and sideswiped the bug.

Through the darkened window Mack saw the

insect thing spin, twist, fall, and bounce right back up.

The second bug had managed to jam a hand, a claw, a whatever-it-was, through the window, which was closing with frustrating slowness.

The limo burned rubber out of the school driveway.

The window shut tight as the car took off. There was a snap like a not-quite-dry twig. The insect hand came loose and hung from the window.

The grasshoppers chased the limo for a few blocks, and if there had been any traffic, they would have caught up.

Fortunately the driver wasn't too concerned with stop signs. The bugs receded and finally gave up the chase as the limo tore through the once-safe streets of Sedona and headed for the desert.

They were well out of town before Mack lowered the window just enough to pull the bug's arm into the car.

"Can I have that?" Stefan asked.

Eleven

A REALLY, REALLY LONG TIME AGO . . .

"What know you of the conjurer's tongue?" the man in mismatched armor asked Grimluk.

"Is it missing?" Grimluk asked.

The man in the mismatched armor—so-called because he wore a helmet that was obviously too large for his rather small head and a chain mail shirt so small it was tied together in the back with pieces of yarn—stared at him as if he were mad. Crazy mad, not angry mad.

"The tongue, fool. The language. Vargran, the tongue of power."

Something about the phrase *the tongue of power* struck Grimluk as funny. He grinned, revealing his five intact teeth.

This proved to be a mistake. The man in the mismatched armor socked Grimluk in the mouth, hard, with an armored fist.

"Not so toothy now, are you?"

"Hey!" Grimluk found the detached tooth heading down his throat. He stopped it by gagging and then spit it out into his hand. "You had no right to punch me!"

"You stupid bumpkin," the man snarled. "Do you think this is some mummer's game?"

Grimluk wasn't sure. He didn't know what a mummer's game might be, and millennia would pass slowly by before Google would be created to answer questions such as this.

"Do you not know that all the world stands as if on the edge of a cliff eleven feet tall? And that all we know and hold dearest is in danger?"

"I know of the Pale Queen."

"You know nothing."

"I have seen her daughter. The Princess. Or so she called herself."

The man in the mismatched armor took a step back. "Do you say that you have seen Princess Ereskigal?" He got a shrewd look on his face, or at least as much of his face as was visible beneath the brim of his helmet. "Tell me of her appearance."

"Very beautiful. With hair the color of a flame. And she ate the head of a terrifying beast like a grasshopper standing on its hind legs."

"Ereskigal!" the man said, and Grimluk saw that his hands shook. "This is dire news. Follow me. Come! You must go before the *gerandon*!"

"What's a *gerandon*?"

"In the Vargran tongue its meaning is 'conclave.' Bumpkin! Do you know nothing?" He set off at a quick walk from the gate of the castle down a winding pathway overshadowed by high stone walls. With each step Grimluk was watched by alert archers who were ready to rain arrows down on him—*into* him, actually—if he made one false move.

The *gerandon* held court in the castle's keep.

Grimluk had never been anywhere so grand. It was at least eleven times more magnificent than the baron's castle. For one thing, there were no farm animals in the room at all. For another thing, the walls were staggeringly tall. They seemed to go up and up forever before culminating in an arched roof that rested on massive buttresses.

At the farthest end of the room was an impressive throne of timber and leather, covered with animal pelts. It was currently unoccupied. It seemed that the king, the usual occupant of the throne, had discovered a pressing need to visit another country. He had discovered this pressing need approximately four seconds after hearing that the Pale Queen was on her way.

In the center of the room was a long, rectangular table. Placed around this table were high-backed chairs, and in the chairs sat a motley assortment of six men and one woman. Grimluk would have guessed even without being told that the men were wizards. All had long beards, varying from wispy and dark to full and gray to patchy and red. The woman did not have a beard, just a slight mustache.

She had to be a witch, Grimluk realized nervously.

There weren't many career paths that could put a woman into a position of power in those days. She was either a witch or a queen, and she didn't look like a queen.

It was she who spoke.

"What interrupts our deliberations?"

The man in mismatched armor jerked a thumb at Grimluk. "This bumpkin—"

"I'm a fleer and a former horse leader, not a bumpkin," Grimluk interrupted.

"This fleer, then, claims to have seen Princess Ereskigal."

Seven sets of eyes, totaling eleven eyes in all (since the woman had but one eye, and one of the men had none), stared at him.

Grimluk gave a brief account of his encounter with the stunning redhead in the forest.

"This is bad, Drupe," one of the men said to the woman.

"How far distant?" the witch Drupe asked Grimluk.

"Two days' walk," Grimluk said.

"Slow and ambling walk?" one of the wizards asked.

"Quick and anxious walking," Grimluk said.

"Once again," the eldest of the wizards said, "I renew my call for the creation of a standardized set of measurements."

"Noted," Drupe said wearily. She took a deep breath and stood up from her chair. She adjusted the patch over her missing eye and stretched a little, like someone who has been sitting too long. "The enemy approaches. Our forces are not ready. We have only eleven of the twelve. Once again we must withdraw, run away from the Dread Foe."

"Ahem," the man in the mismatched armor said.

"Yes?"

"This one here, the bumpkin, says he has the *enlightened puissance*. And he is of age."

Grimluk had been trying his best to sidle back toward the door. He winced as the witch Drupe turned her blazing eye on him.

"Does he indeed?"

"I . . . um . . . You know, when I said I had the . . . the . . . the engorged parlance, I didn't exactly know . . ." He ran out of words at that point. This was not the way he thought it would be. It was normal to exaggerate on a job application, but this had turned suddenly very serious.

The witch came to him. Only then did Grimluk notice that one of her legs was as thick as a tree trunk, gray and leathery, ending in stubby yellow nails.

He couldn't tear his gaze away from the leg.

"It's an elephant leg," Drupe said. She shrugged. "It was a spell gone wrong. I'm working on it."

Grimluk swallowed hard.

"I will give you the simplest of Vargran spells, bumpkin."

"Okay."

"Speak the words as I say them. But as you speak, bumpkin, banish fear from your mind." She waved one hand before his face as though she was pulling away a curtain. "Banish fear and feel instead the blood of your ancestors back through all the generations. Reach back to forgotten time. Summon to you the powers of unyielding earth, drowning water, exhilarating air, and searing, flesh-consuming fire!"

Grimluk didn't want to do any of those things, but it was as if the witch's words were worms eating their way into his very soul. As though her words were within him and no longer without. As though his blood truly did flow with all the strength of his ancestors, all the powers of the world itself.

"Gather to yourself the fearsome wolf and the great eagle, the poison snake and the bludgeoning boar, and speak, *speak*!"

Her face was right in his, her breath on him, her heat warming his body.

Then she opened her hand. And in her palm lay a butterfly. It had been crushed, its wings broken.

"Speak these words, bumpkin: *Halk-ma erdetrad (sniff) gool! Halk-ma! Halk-ma!*"

So Grimluk said the words. He shouted them with all the conviction he could muster.

The butterfly stirred! Its wings moved feebly.

And slowly, slowly, it rose into the air.

Alive!

And then it fell to the floor. Dead again.

"Good enough," Drupe said. She grinned at the amazed wizards. "Good enough."

Twelve

The giant bug arm oozed green-black blood from the stump. It wasn't heavy. It felt like something made out of brittle plastic, the way plastic gets if you leave it out in the sun for a long time.

"It's all yours," Mack said. He handed the arm to Stefan, who hefted it like it might be some kind of weapon.

"My name is Rose Everlast," the Asian woman said. "I'm with the accounting firm of Hwang, Lee,

Chun, and Everlast."

"You're an accountant?" Mack said incredulously. "You don't look like an accountant."

"What do I look like?" Rose asked.

"Hot. Way hot. No offense," Stefan interjected. He was fifteen, after all.

Rose did not seem offended. She opened a leather case on her lap. "We don't have a lot of time." She pulled out two small blue notebooks and handed one to Mack and the other to Stefan.

Mack read the embossed cover. He flipped it open to a picture of him. "This is a passport."

"Yes," Rose said. "It is. You'll notice we've given you a different name. You are now Mack Standerfield. And you," she said to Stefan, "are Stefan Standerfield, age twenty-one."

"Excellent," Stefan said, breaking into a grin. "I can drive!"

"Minors aren't allowed to travel unaccompanied," Rose explained. "Stefan will be your adult older brother."

"Um, whoa. Hold up," Mack said.

Rose ignored him other than to purse her perfect

red lips disapprovingly. "You have a flight to catch. We are running late."

"Hey. I'm not flying anywhere!" Mack said. "I'm going home to kick the golem out of my bedroom and call the FBI or whatever and tell them what's happening."

Rose shrugged. "Then your family will die."

"Stop that, okay?" Mack said.

Rose handed him a credit card. The name on it was Mack Standerfield. "Don't lose this," she said. "Or this." She handed each of them an iPhone.

"Is your number on here?" Stefan asked with a leer.

"I'm a little old for you," Rose said witheringly.

Stefan grinned. "I don't mind."

Rose turned pointedly away from Stefan and gave Mack all her attention. "I've already provided a phone to your golem so he can text you if need be."

"He can text?"

"Of course he can text. He's a golem," Rose said, "not an adult. Now: money. You have a limited budget. You can spend all of it, but once you do, it's gone. If you waste it, you'll have nothing. And remember, you have a long, long way to go."

Mack considered pointing out again that he had no intention of going anywhere. But it was starting to dawn on him that he probably was going. The thing about his mom and dad being killed, that had a realness to it. Nine Iron was an old goof, maybe, but his snakes had been real enough, and that slow-moving blade was sharp enough, too.

And then there were the big giant bug things.

He snapped out of his reveries when he heard the kind of words that tend to snap people out of reveries.

"Did you just say 'one million dollars'?"

"It's not as much as it sounds. You will be paying for air travel, rooms, and food, and all of that is expensive. You may also need to pay bribes. You may find the need to hire assassins. There will almost certainly be medical expenses."

"Medical expenses?" Mack gulped.

Rose closed her leather case, set it aside, and leaned toward him. She smelled of something citrus and yet seductive.

"I haven't been told what all this is about," Rose said. "Not all the details. I only know that the funds come from a Swiss bank account that was first opened in the year 1259."

"That's a long time ago."

"The gold that was used to open the account was in a small strongbox that survives to this day. That strongbox is from an era long, long before even the year 1259. We're talking golden crowns from Ur, rubies from ancient Egypt, diamonds from the empire of Ashoka the Great. Wealth from the four corners of the earth."

"Wow!"

"At one time the contents of that strongbox were worth almost a billion dollars." Rose sighed and sat back. "Unfortunately, the bank used some of that money to invest in shopping malls and hedge funds. So now, all that's left is one million, seven thousand, eight dollars."

"What happened to the seven thousand eight dollars?" Mack asked suspiciously.

Rose smiled and made a sweeping gesture with her manicured hands that encompassed all that was Rose Everlast. "This look doesn't come cheap," she said.

"Totally worth it," Stefan said.

Mack fingered the credit card. "Why me?"

Rose shrugged.

"Do you know an old dead-looking guy named Grimluk?"

Rose shook her head.

"You ever hear of the Nafia?"

"The Mafia?"

Mack shook his head. "Never mind." He glanced at Stefan. "You don't have to do this, dude."

"You're under my wing, man," Stefan said. "That is, like, sacred. Besides—a million bucks?"

Rose drew an oblong folder from the outer zip pocket of the case. "Your tickets."

Mack took them. "Where are we going?"

"I can only tell you the first stop. There you are to find a person, a child like yourself. I don't know who the person is. And I don't know how you are to find this person. My instruction was simply that you go."

"Just go someplace and find some person?" Mack said skeptically. "You realize that makes no sense?"

"Yes. I do. But to be honest, no part of this makes sense to me. But it seems to make sense to those who control this account."

"Well, that's just great," Mack said. "Sorry. I didn't mean to be sarcastic."

"You have to get this person to join you. Together you'll find the next member of the group. And so on."

This both disturbed and reassured Mack. Disturbed because he didn't like meeting new people. Reassured because hopefully this person would be able to explain to him what was going on.

"So where is this kid?" Mack asked.

"Australia."

Mack stared at Rose. He thought of a couple of things to say, none of them polite.

"Sweet," Stefan said, grinning. "I heard kangaroos can box." He interlaced his fingers and cracked his knuckles. "I am going to kick me some kangaroo butt."

DEAR MACK,

HI, IT'S ME, YOUR GOLEM. I'VE DECIDED TO KEEP A
DIARY FOR YOU SO THAT YOU WILL KNOW EVERYTHING
THAT HAPPENED WHILE YOU WERE AWAY.

I WILL CONTACT YOU ONLY IF I HAVE AN EMERGENCY BECAUSE GRIMLUK TOLD ME YOU WOULD BE VERY BUSY FLEEING FROM ALMOST CERTAIN DEATH.

BUT DON'T WORRY: IF YOU SURVIVE, YOU'LL FIND EVERYTHING HERE JUST THE WAY YOU LEFT IT. AND YOU'LL BE ABLE TO READ ALL ABOUT MY ADVENTURES BEING YOU.

YOUR FRIEND,
GOLEM

Thirteen

Mack and Stefan flew from Flagstaff to Los
Angeles without incident. Mack had taken
the trip before, but it was Stefan's first time on a plane.
The idea that cars looked like toys from an airplane
was new to him.

Mack spent his time brooding about the bizarre
turn his life had taken.

Los Angeles International Airport was quite a bit
bigger than the Flagstaff airport, and they got lost while

trying to track down a haunting cinnamon smell. It took them quite a while to locate the Cinnabon, where they tried out the new credit card and found that it worked.

It worked quite well.

So they found a luggage shop and bought two very nice carry-on bags, and then it was off to the Hudson News shop, where they proceeded to fill their new bags with boxes of See's Candy, bags of Cheez-Its, and plenty of sodas. In case they needed a change of clothing, each bought a souvenir T-shirt.

Mack's T-shirt read THE OFFICE. Stefan's read LAPD.

They packed these away. Mack also bought a book, and Stefan bought a magazine with lots of pictures and very few words.

Then they used their iPhones and credit card to sign onto the airport Wi-Fi and downloaded some tunes.

Even after all that, they had a lot of time to kill. The flight didn't leave until ten thirty at night.

So Mack used the time to go online and research the Nafia. He didn't find anything useful.

So he researched *Pale Queen* and came up with a song he'd never heard.

Finally he Googled *Vargran*. There were only a couple of references to a mythical language. But not so much as a word of that language.

No help. It was depressing. If Google didn't have an answer, how was Mack supposed to figure it out?

Finally, it was time to board the plane. They found their seats. Stefan got a window. Mack got a middle seat. The aisle seat was filled by a rather large woman who occupied a good portion of Mack's seat as well.

Mack's anxiety was growing second by second. The ocean—it was right there next to the Los Angeles airport. They would be flying over the ocean for fifteen hours.

Mack had several ways of dealing with his phobias. One was screaming and running away. He was very strongly tempted to do just that.

The other way was to try and talk his way through the fear, using reason and logic and a lot of babble to reassure himself.

"It's just water, there's nothing wrong with water.

Except it's salt water, but who cares about salt, right, that's not the problem, salt, who cares? It's deep that's the problem it's deep deep deep like miles and miles deep so deep that light doesn't even reach the bottom which is full of like glowing radioactive fish monsters of course if you sank that far down you'd already be dead which isn't really very reassuring, is it?"

"What?" Stefan asked.

"Ocean. I don't like ocean. I really, really, really don't like ocean. Because it's, like, so deep, you know? And you can't see what's in it even."

Stefan said, "Huh. We're moving."

"I know we're moving, I can feel the plane rolling, I'm not in a coma, I know we are moving and getting ready to take off and fly straight toward the ocean."

"Probably we won't land in the ocean," Stefan opined.

"Probably? Probably? *Probably* we won't land in the ocean? *Probably?* That's the word you want to use?"

The flight attendant chose that moment to begin the safety lecture. And what was Mack's least favorite part? The part about the life jacket under his seat. That was not helpful.

"Yeah, it'll be totally okay as long as I have a stupid yellow life jacket on and I'm blowing into the stupid tube and then I'll float around the big giant deep cold ocean and I won't drown right away which is great because that way the sharks will have plenty of time to find me and eat me little by little and bite off my foot and I'm screaming and then it bites my butt and then—"

Stefan said, "Sorry, man."

"Sorry?" Mack shrilled, his eyes wild with panic. "Sorry about what?"

Stefan twisted in his seat and socked Mack in the jaw. It wasn't anywhere close to Stefan's strongest punch. In fact, it could be considered an almost friendly punch in the face.

Still, it snapped Mack's head around, stunned him, made his eyes go blurry, and stopped the endless flow of panicky words.

"Thanks," the fat lady said. "He needed that."

The plane was in the air before Mack recovered his faculties.

"Dude—you punched me!"

"You're under my wing, Mack. Can't have you freaking out."

Mack felt his jaw. It still seemed to be attached. But the angle might be off just a bit.

Mack glanced out of Stefan's window. He saw the bright lights of Los Angeles. And he saw the ominous blackness where the land ended and the ocean began.

He closed his eyes tight and gripped the armrest.

How long he sat like that, frozen, he could not know. At some point he fell asleep. While asleep he continued to clutch the armrest.

He woke hungry to find that there was a meal—of sorts—on the fold-down table. Stefan was eating his.

"You've been moaning," Stefan said.

"What was I moaning?"

"'We're going to die,'" Stefan said, and chewed a piece of meat. "You kept moaning it in your sleep."

"What happened to the lady who was sitting here?" Mack asked.

"She found another seat."

Mack felt a little offended. But not much. The screen on the seat back in front of him showed a map with the plane superimposed. Los Angeles was far behind. Sydney, Australia, was much closer but still far ahead.

"How am I going to do this?" Mack wondered aloud. "I'm not exactly a hero."

"Huh," Stefan agreed.

"Once we get to Australia, I'm turning around and going home."

"Back over the ocean?"

"Good point," Mack said miserably.

"I watched a movie," Stefan said. "Put something on, it will distract you."

So Mack watched several movies while clutching the armrests until his fingers were numb and his arms were aching. He also ate a little. The buttered roll was nice.

He slept a little more. And this time he didn't moan about dying. He moaned, but without prophecies of imminent doom.

He woke when Stefan yelled, *"Hey!"* in his ear.

"What? What? What?"

Mack instantly noticed that something was wrong. Everyone on his side of the plane was staring out of the windows, pointing, murmuring.

"Whoa," Stefan said.

Mack didn't want to look out of the window

because if he did, he might see the black ocean, or at least a blackness where the ocean was. But he had to look. Everyone else was, and they didn't sound too happy about what they were seeing.

So Mack looked.

Just beyond the tip of the plane's wing was a small, sleek aircraft like nothing Mack had ever seen or imagined.

It wasn't a jet, that was clear. It had a bulbous front that looked like it was made out of black glass. The bulb was wreathed in what might be steel ivy—like vines, the kind that climb up your porch, but glinting metallically. The vines swept back, twisted into a sort of thick cable, and then swept up to grow around and over something that could arguably be an engine. The engine, if that's what it was, glowed all over with red light that burned bright as a small red sun at the back end.

Taken all together, there was something about the craft that suggested a poisonous plant with a swollen seed on one end and a radioactive root on the other.

The jumbo jet banked sharply left, veering away

from the much smaller pursuer. The floor tilted, the flight attendants yelled, "Seat belts, seat belts!" and one of them pitched over sideways to land in the laps of a couple with a child.

There were screams. There would be more.

Outside, the craft kept pace effortlessly.

The plane righted, steadied. Then, without warning, the floor fell away from Mack as the pilot sent them into a dive. Mack's stomach was in his throat. It was like the first big drop of a roller coaster. And for just a few seconds he was sure he was weightless.

At this point there was more screaming—some of it from Mack.

Meals went flying, drinks toppled, one of the overhead luggage bins popped open and spilled bags.

Outside, the red flower was still right on their wingtip.

As Mack stared in amazement and horror, the door of the pursuer opened, an oval of deep red light in the dark pod. And an inhuman figure appeared, framed there.

And then, despite the fact that both aircraft were flying faster than five hundred miles per hour and were six miles up, the creature leaped.

It landed on the jet's wing, wobbled, then steadied itself.

And it grinned right directly at Mack.

DEAR MACK,

TODAY I ATE PIZZA. BUT I REALIZED THAT I DO NOT HAVE A STOMACH AND HAD TO SPIT IT OUT ON THE TABLE. LATER I USED A SPOON TO REACH INSIDE MY MOUTH AND DIG OUT A STOMACH. I PLACED THE MUD CAREFULLY IN THE TOILET AND FLUSHED MANY TIMES. NOW THERE IS WATER ON THE FLOOR AND ALSO ON THE STAIRS. I THINK MOM NOTICED.

YOUR FRIEND,

GOLEM

Fourteen

A REALLY, REALLY LONG TIME AGO . . .

From the high, crenellated walls of Castle Etruk, Grimluk could gaze down at the endless sea of green trees and fields and see the advance of the Pale Queen's forces. Wherever they went, they burned.

The endless forest was dotted with dozens of small villages. These her forces burned to the ground. They killed and ate the farm animals, killed and didn't eat the men, and enslaved the women and children.

All across the many miles that Grimluk could see, there rose plumes of smoke. The enemy seemed to be advancing from every direction at once. Castle Etruk, which Grimluk had gotten to like over the last couple of weeks, was surrounded.

The town below the castle walls had emptied out. Just about everyone had fled. If Grimluk turned to the east, he could see the last of them disappearing into the forest, rushing from their homes as he had rushed from his. The rumor was that there was a gap in the enemy lines.

Gelidberry and the baby had gone, too. They'd had to move fast, so they took only one cow. And the spoon.

Gelidberry had tried to convince him to take it. "You'll need to eat to keep up your strength."

"No, Gelidberry, I want our baby to inherit the family spoon someday. And if I die . . ."

Soldiers still lined the castle parapet. They were armed with swords and pikes and the occasional bow. But no one expected any of these weapons to stop the army that was coming their way.

Wick, Grimluk's acquaintance from the inn, was among them. He had been promoted to captain of pikes.

But all hope was invested in the Magnifica: the twelve.

Twelve people was not a lot when you actually saw them all together. It was a huge number in the abstract—the only number actually larger than eleven—but when Grimluk looked around him at the shivering, scared mess of young men and women, he was not impressed.

They were seven males and five females. Some were rich, as evidenced by their numerous teeth, their excellent clothing—two of the Magnifica had actual buttons—and their superior education.

The others were poor and wore coarse grain sacks with holes for arms and neck. Some were really poor and wore nothing but strategically placed tufts of grass attached with mud—uncomfortable at the best of times and rather disastrous in a heavy rain.

The wealthiest and best educated of the Magnifica was a woman named Miladew. Despite her station in life, she had befriended a guy named Bruise.

Bruise was poor and ignorant, but he was a capable hunter, as evidenced by the fact that he had a loincloth of black-and-white skunk pelt and fabulous shoes made of the boiled-down skulls of wild boars (complete with tusks).

The boar shoes made a clatter when Bruise walked on the stone parapet, and they were evidently painful, because Bruise cried out softly with each step. The skunk garment had a distinct aroma, but while it could not be described as pleasant, it was far better than the stench that rose from within the castle walls, where butchers tossed hog and cow innards straight onto piles of human poo for the delight of the many, many (many) flies. The butchers would no doubt have tossed leftover food onto the pile as well, but the first leftover would not be developed for many centuries.

"How could the earth be flat and have four corners?" Miladew was saying to Bruise. "Everyone knows the earth has six corners with a giant nail in one of those corners that keeps us attached to the vast bald head of Theramin. Poor Bruise, we really must work on your education."

Bruise nodded and looked sheepish.

The witch Drupe joined them atop the wall. She gazed out at the smoke rising from the forest.

The Magnifica formed a circle around her. She had been their teacher over the long, dread-filled weeks as they struggled to master the Vargran tongue. But no one got very close. Drupe's elephant leg had been replaced by the leg of a giant bird she called an ostrich. The leg was unusually long, and it was feared that Drupe could topple over at any moment.

"Each of you has learned a portion of the Vargran tongue," Drupe said. "Each of you has the *enlightened puissance*. Thus, each of you possesses power that acts by means of Vargran. The power to cause spears to appear and hurl themselves. The power to cause a cold so terrible that hardened soldiers will freeze. The power to move with the speed of a gazelle. The . . ." She noticed many puzzled looks. "It's an animal. Like a deer. But faster."

"Ah," the Magnifica murmured.

"The point is that each of you has magical powers to bring to the approaching—it means 'getting closer'—battle."

A guy everyone called Hungry Hode—his name

was Hode, and he had once mentioned he'd like more than one meal per day—interrupted. "But, Drupe, will we really be able to stop the Dread Foe?"

Drupe looked at him with a mixture of pity and contempt. "With the powers of the Vargran tongue, you will be able to fight the Tong Elves, the Weramin, the Skirrit, the Bowands, the Gudridan—all the many, many (many) fell creatures of the Dread Foe. You may even be able to contest with the princess. But your separate powers will be nothing to the Pale Queen herself."

"Then—" Hungry Hode started to say. But Drupe was on a roll.

"The Dread Foe has all of those powers and more. She can become any creature. She can shrink as small as an ant and swell to a size impossible for your limited minds to comprehend."

Grimluk tried to imagine how big that could be. Horses were big. Cows were big. Did Drupe mean something even bigger? He decided not to ask.

"She can breathe fire!" Drupe cried. "She can cast spells that send mighty stone walls tumbling into dust. She has potions and magic powders. She can command the evil beasts of the forest: snakes, boars, ticks, worms, unicorns, and giant beaver rats."

Grimluk glanced around at his fellow Magnifica. They looked as scared as he felt. None of them knew what Weramin or beaver rats were, but Drupe seemed to think they were very bad indeed.

"Then how?" Grimluk asked, his voice shaky. "How will we defeat the P—I mean, the Dread Foe?"

Drupe stuck out one crooked hand and grabbed him hard by the shoulder. She looked into his eyes. But because Drupe had only the one eye, she chose to stare at just one of Grimluk's eyes. The left one. Not that it matters.

"I don't know," Drupe said.

"Um . . . what?" Grimluk said.

"What does she mean, she doesn't know?" Bruise asked Miladew.

"I know that there is a way," Drupe said. "I know that if the twelve of you can find a way to unite all of your power, all of your courage, into one mighty thrust, you have enough, just barely enough, of the *enlightened puissance* to overcome the P—I mean, the Dread Foe."

She released her hold on Grimluk's shoulder and

hung her head. "It is in the prophecies of the Most Ancient Ones. It is why we have placed all our hopes in you. The twelve of twelve, each filled with the *enlightened puissance*, all twelve united as one, shall stop the Dread Foe."

"'Shall?'" Grimluk echoed hopefully.

"I meant, 'may,'" Drupe corrected.

"Darn," Grimluk said.

Drupe walked a few steps away from them, right to the wall's edge. She stared out at the forest. "Not tonight, but the next night that comes will bring with it the Dread Foe. If we fail . . . then all the wonder of our lives, our happy way of life, the luxury and magnificence, the endless pleasure of our freedom, will be doomed. And all the world will serve the Dr—"

She stopped and clenched her fist and shook it at the ever-approaching smoke.

"No, I will say her name!" Drupe cried in a mix of defiance and fear. "As the final battle approaches, I will speak her name. She comes! She comes! The Pale Queen!"

Fifteen

I t was hard to tell how big it was, the monster on the wing. Maybe not much bigger than a man.

But it was no man.

In the strobe from the jet's wing light, Mack saw a thing covered with sleek, short, copper-colored fur.

The wing monster had two short, stubby legs ending in oversized feet that could almost be human. But its major weight was in the upper body, where it had massive, muscled, broad shoulders supporting a

pair of thick arms. The arms ended in a forest of tentacles. Imagine that the arms were trees—because that's
just about how thick they were—and now imagine
that those trees had been yanked up out of the ground
so that the roots were dangling and waving, all intertwined. These roots, these tentacles were in varying
lengths from a few inches to a few feet.

The wing monster had its stumpy feet planted
uncertainly on the aluminum surface, but the arms
and the tentacles gripped the wing's leading edge quite
securely.

But as bad as the tentacles were—and Mack was
definitely not happy about them—the creature's head
was far worse. Some dark, inexplicable bit of twisted
DNA had decided to reverse the usual location of eyes
and mouth. The eyes—globular, small, startlingly
white, with no sign of a pupil—were below the mouth.
The mouth was filled with an interesting array of teeth.
They looked broken, as if the creature had started out
with a solid wall of big, bright, shiny teeth and then
had broken them randomly with a ball-peen hammer,
leaving jagged crenellations.

When it stared at Mack with its white jelly eyes

and grinned its broken grin, Mack had no doubt, no doubt whatsoever, that it was coming for him.

"Whoa," Stefan said. "Gnarly."

The flight attendants were telling everyone to stay calm. But they didn't look too calm themselves. Anyone could see that the creature was walking its way down the wing toward the plane.

"It's coming to kill me," Mack said, sounding far more calm than he felt.

"You're under my wing," Stefan said. But he sounded a little doubtful to Mack.

"It can't get in, can it?" Mack cried in a shrill, whinnying sort of tone that was definitely not heroic.

"The door can't be opened from the outside," a flight attendant cried, sounding just like Mack had sounded. "Probably."

"I hate *probably*," Mack said. He tried to think of a way out, of a way to fight the monster, or alternately a way to hide. "The bathroom!"

"Yo, I have to go, too," Stefan said, "but we got bigger problems."

"I mean we can hide in there."

Stefan did not argue. Click, click, and their seat

belts fell away. They launched themselves out of their seats and pelted toward the bathroom.

"Sit down!" the flight attendant shouted. "The captain has illuminated the seat belt sign!"

The airplane bathroom was small, but they fit if Mack stood on the toilet. Stefan leaned his back against the door. Mack saw his own reflection in the mirror: he looked scared. Then he noticed how scared Stefan looked, and he got even more scared because Stefan wasn't scared of anything, and if he was scared, Mack knew he himself had better be terrified.

Suddenly from outside the bathroom there were screams.

There was a loud sound and an incredible whoosh that popped Mack's ears. The bathroom door flew open, and the two of them spilled out into the aisle.

The inside of the jet was a madhouse. Paper napkins, peanut bags, plastic cups, purses, magazines and newspapers, and great big hardcover books were flying around as if a tornado had formed inside the plane.

The door—the oval door to the outside—was wide open. Mack saw black night where he should have seen a comforting steel door.

The pressure drop was sucking all the air, and anything not bolted down, straight out through that door. It was as if someone had hooked a massive vacuum cleaner up and cranked it to "deep clean."

Mack glanced to his right. The oxygen masks had dropped, little clear plastic tubes ending in plastic bags that might or might not inflate. People were snatching wildly for the masks, which were being pulled toward the door so that many of them hung almost horizontally and jerked as though they were trying to break free.

Women's hair was swept forward toward the open door. Headphones were yanked from ears and also jerked crazily toward the open door. An entire beverage cart rolled madly down the aisle, slammed a bulkhead, tossed off a Sprite, and was swallowed by that open door. *Shoomp!*

The plane now tilted down, down, down, as if it wanted to plunge straight into the ocean.

Where there were sharks.

Which Mack did not like.

A baby suddenly broke from its mother's arms and went flying toward the door.

Mack leaped, arms outstretched, and snagged the baby by its little blue jumpsuit. But the suction was so strong that the snaps on the Dr. Dentons *pop pop pop*ped and the diapered baby came loose.

Stefan reached past and grabbed the baby's arm, twisted, and managed to hand the baby to Mack before he lost his balance and slid toward the open door.

The suction was lessening now, but only because there was no more air.

Mack breathed in deep and got only a quarter of a lungful of oxygen.

He tried to get back to his seat, back to one of the oxygen masks, back to the screaming, hysterical mother who held out her arms for her baby. But it was an uphill climb now with the plane tilted at a sharp angle.

Mack had to use the legs of the seats almost as a ladder, straddling the aisle, climbing up the steep incline as his lungs sucked on nothing and his vision went red.

He climbed to the mother and, with his consciousness fading, and with it the last of his strength, Mack handed the baby over.

He clambered over the back of a seat—now almost a ledge beneath him—reached, and snagged one of the oxygen masks.

Oxygen was flowing freely. He filled his lungs gratefully and searched for Stefan. Stefan had managed to grab on to a seat in first class and was also sucking oxygen as the plane plunged.

And it was then that the wing monster stepped through the door, tentacle fingers grabbing bulkheads.

It hauled itself all the way in. It bowed its creepy upside-down head but still scraped its slobbery, broken-toothed mouth along the ceiling.

And then the creature did something very strange (like up until this point it had been normal). It began to melt. To change. A sort of black vapor formed a wreath around it, a swirling veil that hid it from sight.

When the smoke cleared, the monster was no more. In its place stood the most beautiful girl Mack had ever seen or ever even imagined.

She had luscious red hair and eyes greener than Mack would have thought possible. Her skin was pale and perfect. Her lips were a dark, dark red.

She stood easily, as though the tilted deck was not even an issue.

She smiled, and it was as if a sun had appeared in the middle of a storm and that sun shone just for Mack, for Mack alone.

"Hello," she said in a laughing, musical voice. "You must be Mack."

Mack sucked on his oxygen mask and wondered in some distant corner of his mind how she could breathe and how she could speak and how the sound waves propagated across a relative vacuum. Because he had learned in science class that sound waves needed air. In fact, he had done an experiment that . . . But that wasn't really important just then because the most beautiful girl in the history of the world was talking to him, just him.

"Hi," he mumbled into his plastic mask. "I'm Mack."

"It's good to meet you, Mack. My name is Ereskigal. My friends call me Risky."

"I'll bet," Mack said.

"Come on, Mack," she said. She held out one perfect, pale, red-nailed hand. "Let's get out of here."

Dear Mack,

I had an excellent day at school. The woman called Ms. Chapman asked me if I was still devouring books. She smiled so I knew this was a good thing. I said that I was. I devoured one for her and she stopped smiling. Then I met the man called Assistant Principal Furman, who asked me what my major malfunction was. I explained to him that I cannot malfunction because I am a supernatural creature made of mud. He told me to go away.

Your friend,

Golem

Sixteen

"I'm good right here," Mack said.

"He's good right here," Stefan said, coming as close as he could while keeping his oxygen mask on.

Risky smiled. It was a dazzling smile. But not really friendly.

The temperature in the plane had dropped like a rock. Mack could see his breath steam around the mask as he exhaled.

"Eng Ereskigal, Arbast," Risky said. *"Eng-ma!"*

And suddenly Mack was up out of his seat and walking like a zombie. Like an old-fashioned zombie, not like one of the cooler *28 Days Later* or *I Am Legend* kind of zombies who mostly ran really fast.

He walked on stiff legs that were not under his control.

Mack knew his legs were not under his control because taking off his oxygen mask and walking into the howling, freezing wind that came in through that awful open door were not things he really wanted to do.

Really, really did not want to do.

But his legs were moving just the same.

And Risky was grinning.

Mack gasped at thin air. More air than before— it wasn't completely airless now that the plane had dropped somewhat—but it was like trying to fill your lungs after a long run while breathing through a straw.

"No!" Mack yelled, not that his voice carried very far. Somehow Risky could make herself heard just fine despite the lack of oxygen, but Mack sounded like he was a squeaking mouse.

Mack's mouth cried, "No!" but his legs and feet said, "Let's go!"

Risky leaned close to him, her face just inches from his. She smelled like dark woods at night, and like the perfume counter at Macy's, and a little like Mack's aunt Holly, who lived in a converted school bus on a communal farm in Mendocino.

It was an intoxicating smell.

"Poor Mack," Risky said. "Did you really think you could be one of the Magnifica? Did you think you would rush around heroically and stop my mother from retaking all that is hers?"

Mack didn't really have a good answer to that. Because he wasn't really listening. He was marching his lead feet toward the open door, and now he was so close he could reach out a hand and try to grab the frame and try to stop himself, but he couldn't, he couldn't, and his fingers were slipping, and OMG, he could look straight down and see moonlight sparkling off the waves miles and miles below.

"*Odaz,*" Risky whispered. Then, in a shout of triumph, "*Odaz-ma!*"

And Mack was now in the doorway itself, hands

gripping the sides, toes already hanging, like a surfer hanging ten. The wind was beating him up, making his cheeks vibrate, his hair froth, his eyes water.

Risky was behind him now. He felt her hand against his back.

"No way!" Stefan yelled, although his voice sounded as squeaky as Mack's had. Mack glanced back and saw Stefan swinging something big and black.

Stefan hit Risky in the back of the head with someone's carry-on bag.

Risky staggered forward, nearly pushing Mack out of the door. But Mack moved fast. He detached one hand, swung around, grabbed Risky by her wondrous red hair, and tripped her over his leg and out the door.

Risky fell through the door.

But even as she fell, she struck out with one arm, one arm that was now the branched, tentacled arm of the monster.

The tentacles completely imprisoned Mack's free arm. The pressure of the five-hundred-mile-per-hour wind dragged at Risky, and she dragged at Mack. Stefan wrapped his strong arms around Mack and tried to hold on, but it was no good, no good at all.

Mack lost his grip. He flew out of the door.

The wing flashed by beneath him, the tail flashed by, a huge scythe. It barely missed him, and then Mack was tumbling and spinning and screaming as he fell through the night.

Stefan had released his grip, but it was too late to save himself. Now as Mack spun crazily through the air, he saw flashes of Stefan, his arms windmilling: a crazy windblown action figure twirling out of control.

And Risky fell, too, her clothing billowing comically, her red hair a tornado. She laughed as she fell. Mack couldn't hear it over the hurricane howl of wind, but he could see her mouth.

They were all three close, within a few dozen feet of each other.

The jet, on the other hand, was already far away and far above. Rushing away from them at five hundred miles per hour.

Mack saw moonlit sky and silvery clouds. He saw dappled ocean far below. In the east the sun was peeking up over the curve of the earth. And in the other direction he could just make out what must be a city's lights—Sydney, no doubt.

The ocean that he had feared for so long was now rushing up to crush him like a windshield hitting a bug.

Sharks would eat whatever was left.

Seventeen

"Nooooooooo!" Mack screamed, but the wind tore the words right out of his mouth.

The plane had been cruising about seven miles up. It had dropped since losing pressure, but when Mack was yanked from the jet, it was still four miles up.

Mack recalled reading once that the fastest something could fall was about 120 meters per second. Which was pretty fast. In fact, it was about 268 miles per hour.

If he'd had access to his computer so he could use Wolfram|Alpha, Mack might have figured out that he didn't have a lot of time.

But of course he had a more immediate problem: very little air.

Just as Mack lost consciousness, he saw the smaller craft, Risky's weird flying seedpod, come sweeping in at a strangely slow speed. It seemed to be coming to a stop in midair. But that, Mack knew, might be an illusion.

Mack blacked out.

But as he fell toward the ocean and back into the earth's air, he revived. He swam up through layers of clinging unconsciousness. For those first few seconds he was lost, not knowing what had happened or where he was.

The truth was a stab in the heart.

He cried out in terror.

He was much closer to the ocean. Fifteen thousand feet. There was air at fifteen thousand feet, but it was still incredibly cold.

Which was not going to be a problem for very long.

If you know what we mean.

He had time to scream once more, and he did, but his brain was working at desperate speed. How to survive a fall from four miles up?

Answer: no way.

Gravity had hold of him and was determined to smash him into the water that would be as hard as concrete at this speed.

He needed time to think! He needed to stop falling. To stop everything, because if he didn't stop everything he was dead at the age of twelve, a pulpy mess to be eaten by sharks, his bones to be coated with coral.

He needed to stop time.

He could see individual waves now, fluorescing in the starlight, the tallest tips just touched with pink sunrise.

"Ret click-ur!"

That's what Mack shouted, with eyes closed, his body clenched tight for the impact that would snap his bones and pop him open like a water balloon. The words bubbled up out of some pocket of memory, a once heard and almost forgotten phrase in a tongue he did not recognize or know.

The wind stopped. That was the first thing he noticed.

The wind stopped.

He pried one eye open. The waves were still there, still below him. And so close below him, so close he could smell the salt.

But they were not getting *closer*.

Mack hung in midair, balled up as if he were hoping to cannonball and make a big splash and then swim back to the diving board.

His body was trembling, shaking so hard from cold and fear he thought the shaking might pop his shoulders out of their sockets.

Amazingly, the ocean was no longer rushing toward him at four times the speed limit on most freeways.

Mack twisted his head around. He saw stars. And outlined by those stars, Stefan. The bully of all bullies was hanging in midair, just like Mack.

The girl, Risky, was nowhere to be seen. Neither was the bizarre craft Mack now recalled slowing down and coming to a near stop.

"Huh," Stefan said.

"We're alive," Mack whispered. "It worked."

"What worked?" Stefan asked calmly.

"I just said the words that the old dude—Grimluk—said when he made everything stop."

Stefan thought about that for a while and said, "Huh." Then, "Now what?"

Mack wasn't ready to think about "now what?" His heart was still trying to beat its way out through his ribs. His stomach was about twenty thousand feet behind him. His entire body was shaking like the rough-road simulator in an arcade racing game.

"How high up do you think we are?" Mack asked.

"Not as high as we were," Stefan said reasonably. "Probably if we dropped from this high we wouldn't get totally squashed."

Mack peered through the darkness all around. He could clearly see the coastline, with the bright lights of Sydney and all its suburbs spread in a north-south line.

And in the other direction the sun was definitely coming up and pushing the darkness back. In fact, it was kind of pretty in a pinkish, pale purple kind of way.

"Here's the thing," Mack said when he had regained his composure. "I don't exactly know how to turn it off. The spell or whatever it is."

"Huh," Stefan observed.

"Maybe I need a whole different thing to say. But I have this feeling Grimluk just said the same thing over again. You know, like if you push a power button to turn something on, you turn it off by pushing the same button. Right?"

"Huh."

"The thing is, though, we kind of stopped time or whatever, so—"

"You stopped time, not me," Stefan said, sounding like he was trying to avoid responsibility.

"So, if I start it up again, do we go back to what we were doing?"

"Sure."

"Falling?"

"Yeah," Stefan said, "but we wouldn't be falling as far."

"It's not distance I'm worried about," Mack said. "It's speed. What if we kept all the speed we had before?"

Stefan had no answer and neither did Mack. But at that moment he noticed something: a sailboat. It was floating along on the breeze not far below and not far away.

"I think our ride's here," Mack said. "I'm going to try it."

"What about the . . . eh, never mind. Whatever," Stefan said.

"Ret click-ur!"

Mack yelled it.

Gravity reached up and snatched him again.

It dragged him straight down. He hit the water hard. Hard enough to squeeze the air from his lungs. Hard enough to sting. It felt like a really bad session of dodgeball.

He plunged deep. Deeper than he'd ever been in a swimming pool. Down and down, and it seemed like he would never stop.

He kicked and thrashed and headed for the surface, which was a silvery barrier so very high above him.

Lungs screaming, heart pounding, he went up and up, but sooooo veeeeery slooowly.

Then, all at once, his head was out of the water and

he sucked in warm, damp air.

Stefan was treading water close by. "Dude—we just fell out of a plane and we're still alive!"

"But we're in the ocean!" Mack cried.

"No big deal. The water's not that cold."

"It's still the ocean. The *ocean*!"

"It's just water, man. Chill. What are you so scared of?" Stefan asked.

"That!" Mack said, and pointed.

He pointed at the gray, triangular fin that sliced through the water, turned, and came straight for him.

DEAR MACK,

I AM SORRY ABOUT . . . WELL, YOU'LL SEE WHEN YOU GET BACK. I TRIED TO TEXT YOU, BUT I GUESS YOU WERE BUSY OR DIDN'T HAVE A SIGNAL. ANYWAY, DON'T WORRY: IT'S TOO LATE NOW.

YOUR FRIEND,

GOLEM

Eighteen

"*R*et *click-ur!*"

Mack yelled it and got a mouthful of salt water.

He yelled it again.

But the shark fin kept coming. Nothing stopped. Nothing changed.

"Huh," Stefan remarked.

"Aaaaaah!" Mack cried. He'd always known it would end this way.

The fin disappeared beneath a swell that lifted Mack up like a cork. He felt something big brush against him. It turned him around. He cried out in terror and started swimming, splashing, heedless of direction so long as it was away.

But then the fin! It was in front of him. Coming straight at him, fast, fast, so fast!

Then the shark rolled over onto its side. Mack was staring straight into the shark's evil eye.

Only it didn't look evil. And instead of a huge gaping mouth full of razor-tipped teeth, Mack saw a quirky smile.

It took several seconds for the truth to percolate through Mack's brain. It was not a shark.

"It's a dolphin," Mack yelled to Stefan.

Stefan yelled back, "Sharks are way cooler."

"What?"

"Didn't you ever see *Megashark vs. Giant Octopus*? That was so cool the way the shark, like, ate that whole bridge."

Not for the last time, Mack wondered if he and Stefan were even from the same planet.

Then something much bigger than the dolphin

appeared. A vast white sail. It was closer to Stefan than to Mack. They both started shouting and yelling.

Stefan yelled, "Yo!"

Mack yelled, "Save me! Save me! Help! For the love of God rescue me!"

The sail—they couldn't see the actual boat because it was hidden by the swells—suddenly collapsed. And then they could see the boat itself, the blue hull with chrome railings. It was turning toward them, slowing but coming closer.

A man stood at the wheel. He was barely visible in the dim light, but Mack could see the glow of a cigar.

They swam hard for the boat, which was now just a few dozen yards away. Mack was pretty sure he would be chomped by a shark before he could get aboard. But he was going to give it a try.

The man came to the rail and tossed them a rope. Stefan grabbed it and carried it to Mack, who clutched it like it was his last hope of life. Which it probably was.

A minute later they were hauled up the side and stood, wet and shaky but definitely alive, on the teak deck of the sailboat.

"Out for a swim, then?" the man asked, in what Mack assumed was an Australian accent.

Mack stared at him.

"Bit of a haul to Sydney Harbour, mate," the man said.

"Yes," Mack said, spitting out salt water. "I guess we didn't think it through."

"Well, you're young," the man said. "We were all young once, eh? Right. Then we'll get you dried off. Get you a bite. We'll be all snug in our slip in a couple hours."

"Thanks," Mack said. "You saved our lives."

"Don't thank me. Thank my daughter. She's the reason we were looking for you."

"You were . . . what?"

"Go on below, she'll explain it all to you. And maybe you can get her to cook you an omelet."

Stefan led the way down the narrow stairs to the cabin. Here was light and warmth and the smell of food. Mack could almost—not quite—forget that he was on a tiny vessel in the midst of a vast ocean filled with sharks.

A girl sat at a cramped table. She had dark skin,

incongruously blond hair pulled into a ponytail, and brown eyes. She was drinking a cup of coffee, gulping it—not sipping.

She looked up at them with no sign of surprise. "Which one of you is it?"

Stefan, fully recovered despite still being wet and having a piece of seaweed draped over one shoulder, said, "It's me."

The girl cocked her head to one side. Then she laughed. "Don't waste your time flirting with me, mate. You're a fine-looking fellow, no mistaking that. But I'm not looking for a fine fellow, I'm looking for a *magnificent* fellow."

She looked shrewdly at Mack. Like he might be worth something but still wasn't quite what she'd been hoping for.

"You'd be the one," she said. She half stood, reached out her hand, and Mack shook it. He felt calluses. This was not a girl who obsessed over moisturizing. She had done lots of physical work in her life. Mack noticed things like that. Her shoulders were strong; her gaze was direct and not even a little shy.

"My name's Jarrah Major," she said.

"I'm Mack. This is Stefan."

"Have a seat, boys. Don't worry about the wet clothes; you'll dry soon enough."

Mack sat. He was still stunned and scared and feeling a little stupid. "Your dad said you were looking for us. How did you . . ."

Jarrah laughed. "Long story short, I'm the girl you've come here to find. I'm the second of the twelve."

Nineteen

One of the rules of Great Literature is: show, don't tell. But one of the other rules of Great Literature is: don't go on and on with boring scenes where nothing happens but a lot of talking.

So let's just have a quick glance at what Jarrah told Mack and Stefan on the way into stunning Sydney Harbour, and then move on, shall we?

Jarrah's father, Peter Major, was a journalist. A "journo," as she said. He was also an avid sailor. Which is only important because that's how Jarrah came by the boat she took to meet Mack as he fell from the sky.

Jarrah's mother is more important to the story because she was an archaeologist who was leading the first ever expedition *inside* Uluru.

Uluru was a gigantic rock in the middle of the Australian Outback (no, not Outback the restaurant chain, Outback as in the vast Australian desert).

No one even knew there was an inside to Uluru. Until Jarrah's mother, Karri. *Karri* and *Jarrah* were both Indigenous names. *Karri* meant a type of eucalyptus. And so did *Jarrah*.

Using all the latest ground-penetrating radar and other hi-tech toys, Karri Major had discovered a network of caves deep within Uluru. Being an Indigenous Australian herself, and a member of a local clan, she was able to convince her people that it would not be sacrilege to drill a small tunnel to reach those caves.

Which she did.

As soon as they docked, Jarrah's father drove them to Sydney Airport. Mack and Stefan had to be careful at the airport because the plane they'd been snatched out of had landed. There were reporters and cops and just mobs of milling people all around as the spokesman for the airport explained that something very unusual had happened on the flight.

Yes; very unusual.

Mack and Stefan were listed as missing. Turning up alive and well right then would just delay things for hours.

"Problem is," Jarrah's dad said, "it's a long wait for the plane to Ayers Rock."

Ayers Rock being Uluru. Same place, different name.

"If we hang out here, we'll be spotted," Mack said, shielding his face with his hand as if he were in bright sunlight. (He wasn't; he was in an airport, remember?)

"There's no other way," Jarrah said.

"Unless we got a private jet," Mack said.

Jarrah's father made a dismissive sound. "Those don't come cheap."

Mack pulled out his credit card with a flourish. "I got it covered."

The private jet was extremely cool. Tall leather

seats that reclined all the way back. Thick carpeting. An excellent choice of movies. And a small buffet laid out with cheese, crackers, shrimp, some kind of pinkish dip, and sodas.

They left Jarrah's father at the airport and took off for Uluru.

Mack had intended to keep his eyes peeled for Risky's creepy flying machine. But it had been a very long and sleepless night. He was more tired than he would have believed possible. Falling from an airplane and landing in the ocean will take a lot out of you.

He woke when the plane started to descend toward a very basic-looking airport. Barely an airport, really. Just a single paved strip and two low-slung buildings surrounded by a vast red emptiness.

It was as if someone had taken a billion red bricks, ground them to dust, and then spread them over a million square miles. There were trees, but they were widely spaced. And just a single road.

It struck Mack that he was very, very far away from home. He'd never been this far from home. He'd stayed with his grandparents in Michigan once for about three days while his parents went off doing . . .

well, whatever it was parents did when they ditched their kids.

He supposed they would miss him. If they even noticed he was gone. The golem wasn't exactly a perfect copy, but it would probably be good enough to fool his parents.

"I think I'm homesick," Mack said.

"Of course you are; who wouldn't be?" Jarrah said.

"I wouldn't be," Stefan said. He yawned. "It's good to get out of the house."

"It's not like we're going to the park to play Frisbee," Mack grumped.

Stefan laughed. "Yeah, this is way better."

It occurred to Mack that maybe Stefan's home life wasn't everything it could be.

"Looks desolate, doesn't it?" Jarrah said. She was friendly at least. That was good. If Mack was going to save the world from some evil villain with a very beautiful but crazy-bad daughter, it would be best to have pleasant people along with him.

"It looks a little like home," Mack said. "I'm a desert rat myself. Arizona."

"Ha," Jarrah said. "Your desert's all full of roads and cities. Civilized, like. The Outback's a bit different. Emptiest place on earth, you know. Millions of square miles of nothing much." She glanced over at Stefan. "You two been friends for long, then?"

"Actually, Stefan was my bully. But we've moved on."

Stefan jerked a thumb at Mack. "He saved my life."

This seemed to impress Jarrah, who gave Mack a long, appraising look as the plane spiraled down toward the tiny airport.

"You don't look so much like a great hero," Jarrah said.

"I'm pretty sure I'm not," Mack said wearily. "My throat is hoarse from screaming in terror. I don't think heroes have that problem."

The plane landed without incident. Waiting outside the terminal was a tall, very thin woman with springy black hair and very dark skin.

"Mack, my mum. Mum, Mack. And this is Stefan. Mack's bodyguard." Her Australian accent turned *bodyguard* into *bodygaad*.

Karri Major was covered in the red dust Mack had seen flying in. She was dressed in cargo pants and a vest with an awful lot of pockets. Webbing straps hung from various places holding various instruments: small hammer, steel file, a soft brush, a camera, a flashlight.

"So you're the boy from the sky," Karri said. She looked at Mack with something like awe—like she was gazing upon a miracle or meeting the Dalai Lama.

"Come on then," she said, and gave him a sort of shoulder bump that seemed a bit weird coming from an adult.

Mack said, "Yes, ma'am," mostly because he couldn't think of anything else to say.

They went to the parking lot, where Karri led the way to a sort of dune buggy. It was yellow, but so covered in red dirt that no more than six square inches of paint was actually visible. It looked like it had been made out of an SUV but with a platform on the back and a winch on the front and big, oversized tires. A rack of spotlights perched on top.

The buggy made a very satisfying roar.

They drove peacefully from the airport out into the desert, windows down. After just a few minutes Karri pulled off the highway onto a dirt road. She stopped the car and climbed out.

"I have work to catch up on," Karri explained. She pulled a rugged laptop from a rucksack and traded places with Jarrah. Jarrah sat behind the steering wheel, which was on the wrong side, the right side, the Australian side.

Mack assumed they would be sitting there for a while. But then Jarrah turned the key, turned to look over her shoulder, and winked at Mack. "Hold on, mate; this gets a bit bumpy."

"Wait. You're driving?" Mack asked in a voice he hoped didn't sound too terrified.

"No worries," Karri said. "Jarrah's been driving in the bush for years. Ever since she was nine."

"Yeah, no worries," Jarrah said.

Then she shoved the shift knob forward and stomped on the gas. The buggy roared and shot down the dirt road. It took off like some giant had kicked it.

"A bit bumpy" was an understatement. Mack felt like he'd been dumped into a blender set on "vibrate to death."

The dirt road was edged by occasional bushes that smacked the sides of the buggy as it went past. A cloud of dust billowed behind them.

"H-h-h-o-o-o-w-w-w-w f-f-f-a-a-a-r-r-r i-i-i-s-s-s i-i-t-t?" Mack asked. It was hard to talk without unclenching his teeth, and when he unclenched his teeth they vibrated so hard he thought he might break one.

"Not far," Jarrah said. For some reason she didn't seem to vibrate quite as much. "Not far" came out as "Naw faa."

Jarrah grinned, raised her eyebrows, and sent the buggy flying, absolutely airborne, off a red dune. They landed with a spine-shortening crunch amid scruffy bushes and kept right on going.

"Look!" Stefan shouted. He grabbed Mack's shoulder and squeezed.

Mack looked. There, off to the left side, two kangaroos were speeding along, bounding on their giant hind legs as if they were racing the buggy.

In spite of the pounding he was taking, Mack smiled. All right: kangaroos. How cool was that?

"Can we pull over?" Stefan asked.

"You want to take a picture?" Jarrah asked.

"No. I want to box them," Stefan said.

Jarrah looked at Mack in the rearview mirror and smiled broadly. "I like your bully."

She kept driving at breakneck speed, and the kangaroos fell behind. But suddenly she stopped. She turned off the car engine and popped open the door.

"Why are we stopping?" Mack asked.

"Because you should see this," Jarrah said. "It's where we're going. It's why you didn't just drown out in the deep blue sea. It's Uluru, mates—Uluru."

DEAR MACK,

DID YOU KNOW THAT YOU CANNOT EAT CATS? EACH DAY I LEARN A LITTLE MORE. SO I THINK I AM BECOMING A BETTER AND BETTER MACK. BUT IT'S POSSIBLE THAT I HAVE GROWN MORE THAN I SHOULD BECAUSE MOM WAS WHISPERING TO DAD THAT I NEEDED A SHRINK.

YOUR FRIEND,

GOLEM

Twenty

A REALLY, REALLY LONG TIME AGO...

They surrounded the castle like a sea: the creatures of the Pale Queen. Grimluk had seen some ugly in his life, but this was more ugly in one place, all together, than he could ever have imagined.

The Skirrit were the most numerous. They advanced in well-ordered columns, armed with wickedly curved blades like scythes. They swung these upward since that was how their insect arms worked best. They were quick and accurate and deadly.

"Be ready, brothers and sisters," Grimluk commanded the other eleven. Although he had been the last to arrive, Grimluk had demonstrated a quick grasp of the basics of Vargran. And he had managed on more than one occasion to combine his power with that of others.

The Magnifica had not yet combined all their powers. Drupe had warned them that such an event might destroy them all as well as the Pale Queen. Some believed it would destroy the entire world, such would be the power needed to stop the Pale Queen.

The Tong Elves moved as clans, independent bands incapable of organization, each led with a branch of some particular tree. There were Pine Tong Elves and Birch Tong Elves and Oak Tong Elves. For weapons, the elves preferred bats and sticks, sometimes enhanced with chips of sharpened stone driven into the ends.

Near Deads, of course, were even less organized than elves and tended to wander around more or less at random looking for some living thing to eat. Sometimes they would free themselves for a moment or two from the spells that controlled them, and then they were perfectly capable of eating a Skirrit or a Bowand.

The terror of the Near Deads was that it was very difficult to actually kill them. They were human, not really different from Grimluk, except for being dead and possessed of a powerful hunger for human flesh. But the Pale Queen's spells had been layered upon them in such a way that even a headless Near Dead would keep moving forward, grabbing what it could and attempting, rather stupidly, to eat without benefit of head or mouth.

"Remember that we are not tasked to fight Skirrit or Bowands or even Gudridan," Miladew said for all to hear. "We must go toward the Dread One herself."

"It will mean going through all of these," Bruise said, sweeping his hand wide to indicate the sea of monsters.

"Yes," a fellow named Chunhee said with relish. "Through them!"

Chunhee was the most bloodthirsty of the Magnifica. He had come the farthest, from a land of dragons and eating sticks.

Drupe joined them. She touched Grimluk's

shoulder lightly to let him know she was behind him. "Keep your eyes open, my brave twelve of twelves. You will know the Dread Foe's location by the light she will reveal when she is ready to strike."

It seemed as if the world was poised then, as though the great disk of the planet had come loose and was tipped on the edge of a cliff. Grimluk's breathing came hard. He wished with all his heart that he could be with Gelidberry and the baby. Even the cows would be comforting now.

Then, suddenly, it was as if a second sun was rising. A red light, bloodred, bubbled up like ooze, like thickened mare's blood, from the direction that would one day be called south.

"There!" Drupe cried, and pointed.

Every one of the enemy felt it instantly. It was as if they had been struck by lightning. They did not advance, they leaped! They did not march, they raced! A single spasm launched every Bowand, every Skirrit, every Tong Elf, every Dredge and Gudridan and Near Dead and Blood Bat forward like arrows from a bow.

The walls of the castle shook from the sheer impact.

Bowands fired their poisoned darts from their slimy, sinewed arms.

Bruise held up his hands and cried, *"Marf ag chell!"*

The falling darts changed in midair. When they fell, they were crumbs of bread.

"Nice," Grimluk said to Bruise.

Unfortunately Bruise's Vargran was not powerful enough to protect many beyond the Magnifica. On both sides of them the Bowand darts found their targets. The poison darts sank deep into neck and shoulder and chest. And the venom worked its terrible magic, causing strong men to flee from terrors unseen. Some leaped from the battlements in panic.

"To the gate!" Grimluk cried.

The twelve raced down from the battlements, down the narrow stone stairways, which shook beneath their feet. Awestruck soldiers parted to let them pass.

The gate was built of massive tree trunks. It was as powerful as any physical thing could be. Nevertheless, it would stand for only a few more minutes before the onslaught.

Pikemen and archers, trained for just this moment,

formed a semicircle around the Magnificent Twelve. Ten strong men had been given the job of swinging the gate open. Drupe and two other great witches would be there to help them close it again. But they all knew that it would be a near thing and the enemy would pour through even as the twelve rushed out.

All stood at the ready.

Miladew smiled a shaky smile and nodded at Grimluk. "Lead us, Grimluk."

Grimluk closed his eyes and formed a picture of Gelidberry and the baby. It suddenly occurred to him that he had a good name for the baby.

"Victory," Grimluk said.

"Victory or death!" Bruise shouted.

"Yeah," Grimluk said less enthusiastically. "Or death."

Then, in a clear if nervous voice, he cried, "Throw open the gate!"

The gate wasn't so much thrown open as hauled.

Vargran spells flew. The enemy surged. And Grimluk led the Magnificent Twelve straight into the teeth of foes as numerous as the stars.

Twenty-one

Looming ahead, larger and larger, was the rock. Ayers Rock. Uluru.

It sat there like the world's biggest blood blister. All around, in every direction, the land was flat. But there, for no good reason, was this massive, incredible brown-red rock.

If by "rock," you mean "mountain." Or at least, "squashed, flat-topped mountain."

"They say it just dropped out of the sky," Jarrah

explained, shouting to be heard.

"Who says?"

"The people it belongs to. The people who lived here long before Europeans showed up. Mum's people. My people, too, partly."

Karri looked up from her laptop to say, "It's an inselberg. It's what's left after a much bigger mountain has eroded. It's the hard core of an ancient mountain. The real mystery is not how the rock got here, but how the people did."

"Why is that a mystery?" Mack asked.

"The Indigenous peoples have been here for at least forty thousand years. You may have noticed Australia's an island. So how did they get here thousands of years before anyone had learned to sail? And once they got here, why did they seem to forget how to use the sea? Why did they come to live in the most desolate place on earth?"

Mack pondered this while he stared at the rock. They were moving again, getting closer. Jarrah was driving at a somewhat more reasonable speed, and they were now circumnavigating the rock.

"It seems . . . ," Mack started to say. Then he

couldn't think of quite what it seemed.

"It seems familiar," Jarrah said.

"Yeah," Mack agreed, surprised.

"Like it's something you remember but you've never seen it before. Like maybe it was in some dream you had and forgot. But even that's not quite it. More like this place is deep down inside your head. Like it's down in your DNA."

"Yeah. That's exactly it," Mack said, frowning.

Jarrah winked at him. "Most people—people who aren't complete nongs, anyway—feel that way."

They stopped when they reached a small camp. There were three dusty tents and half a dozen vehicles. The camp was at a respectful distance from the thousand-foot-high wall of Uluru.

It was hot out, but nothing Mack hadn't experienced before. Uluru was rushing toward a setting sun, and the rock surface glowed redder than before. Up close it wasn't as smooth as Mack had expected. In places it looked as if the rock had been sandblasted, like some giant had set out to etch the surface and stopped before revealing any sort of pattern.

"Is this where we're going?" Mack asked.

"No, this is just our base camp. We're going up there." Jarrah pointed toward the top of the rock. "The Indigenous people dislike folks climbing on it. It hurts them. Like watching someone tread on the flag, I suppose. Tourists do it anyway, but this is a sacred place."

"Like skateboarding in a church," Stefan said, tilting his head back.

Mack noticed Jarrah's eyebrows go up, admiring Stefan's metaphor. Mack suspected it wasn't a metaphor at all, but something Stefan had actually done.

"But we have permission," Jarrah's mother said, "because we're not skateboarding in church, we're learning about the church, discovering it."

"We have to climb up there?" Mack said dubiously.

"It's not so bad," Jarrah said.

It was so bad, despite a rope handrail that had been set up in places. They climbed inside a deep crease in the rock face, and in places the cleft was so narrow that Mack had to beware of scraping his shoulders.

By the time they reached the top, Mack was exhausted and his thighs ached and his knees were wobbly. He liked to think he was in decent shape, but he was in decent shape for gym class. Not in decent shape for running from Skirrit, flying clear across the planet, falling from several miles up into the ocean, and then climbing a thousand-foot wall.

Still, the view from the top was stunning. The sun was split by the horizon and sent out crazy streamers of brilliant red and yellow across a boundless sky.

"Nice, eh?" Jarrah asked. "Come on, then, better to reach the shaft while we still have light."

Uluru was about three miles long, a sloping table-top, pitted and sliced, but overall it looked fairly flat. The shaft was not far away, easily spotted because it was topped by a frame with a winch and a motor.

Mack stepped cautiously to the edge of the shaft. It went straight down, a nearly round hole with no light coming from inside.

Mack could feel his inner fear sensor begin to ring urgently. Already his breathing was constricted, his throat closing up, his heart pounding in some not-quite-rhythmic way.

"When we get down, we'll turn on the lights," Karri said.

"Get down?" Mack asked in a shrill voice. "Wait a minute. You think we're going down there? Down there? Down a black hole in a massive rock where I'll be totally surrounded by billions of pounds of rock and it will be all around me like I'm buried alive?"

"We have a sort of basket on a winch. You climb in, hold on to the grip, and down you go. Nothing to it, really," Jarrah said.

"Ah-ha-ha no. No, no, no, no," Mack said. "No. No, nonononono."

Karri and Jarrah both stared at him, puzzled.

"You're not claustrophobic, are you?" Karri asked.

"I'm not?" Mack shrilled. "Yes. Yes, of course I am. I have, like, a really strong dislike for the idea of being buried alive under some giant mystical rock in Australia!"

Jarrah shrugged. "I thought you'd want to see what Mum found."

"Me? No. Pictures will be fine. Or even just a description," Mack said. "Because there is no way, no, no, no, no way. No. Way.

"No.

"No way.

"My point is: no."

"Well then, this whole trip is a bit of a waste then," Jarrah said, clearly disappointed. "I mean, I could have shown you pictures back in Sydney."

"Yes. Well. No one mentioned we were going to drop down a shaft into the bowels of the earth," Mack pointed out.

"Fair enough," Jarrah admitted. "I don't suppose you could—"

"No. Whatever you're going to say, the answer is no," Mack said.

"How about—"

"No."

"But if we—"

"No."

"What are those?" Stefan asked.

"What are what?" Mack asked. But even as he asked, he saw what Stefan meant. Which did not mean he could answer the question.

Because what he saw, he had never seen before.

They were outlined against the setting sun, perhaps two dozen of them in all. They seemed small, maybe no taller than Mack himself. You might almost think they were children, but their shape was wrong.

And the way they moved was wrong.

Karri pulled a flashlight from one of her many pockets. She aimed the beam. It illuminated a triangular face dominated by the oversized eyes of a night creature. The nose was a slit. The ears were pointed— Vulcan ears, but swept forward at the points.

The mouth grinned in a sort of tight V shape. The V grin was lined with teeth that stuck out beyond the lips. Not like buck teeth, but curved, like overgrown fingernails—like talons, but talons that were teeth.

There would be time later (Mack hoped) to figure out just how to describe those teeth.

The flashlight beam shook as Karri played it down the creature's body to highlight a strangely quaint little outfit: red leather shorts held up with green suspenders over a sort of spangled vest.

They had overly long arms that dragged their long, delicate fingers on the ground as they walked.

The legs were bare, and that was unfortunate because they looked a great deal like goat legs, with curly tan-colored hair similar to that which spilled from under the creatures' jaunty green caps.

"Who are you? And what are you doing here?" Karri asked.

"You don't speak; we speak."

They had surprisingly deep voices, for child-sized freaks of nature.

"Get off this rock," Karri said bravely. "You're not allowed up here."

Mack guessed that "you're not allowed" wasn't going to quite do it.

Sure enough.

"Shut your vile, filthy, fruit-chewing mouth, you low, slow, soggy bag of water; you sweat-oozing, cheese-scented wad of pulp mounted on toothpicks; you barely animated mistake of nature." One of them delivered this peroration (a word Mack had gotten wrong in a spelling bee). The creature stabbed the air with his long, thin fingers and almost spit as he spoke.

"I am here by right," Karri said. "Now shove off."

"Yeah, shove off," Jarrah echoed her mother.

Mack was impressed by their courage. The creatures were not.

"We are elves of the Gum Tree Tong," the

spokesman said, with pride and arrogance that really should have been matched to someone bigger. "We will have what we came for, you pus-filled, slobber-stained blood balloon!"

And with that, all of the elves of the Gum Tree Tong—whatever that was—rushed forward.

Twenty-two

"Ahhhhh!" Mack cried, knowing even as he made that whinnying sound that he was confirming his unsuitability as a hero.

Stefan said, "If I can't box kangaroos, I'll pound me some elves," and struck a defensive combat pose in full G.I. Joe mode.

Three of the elves were on him in a heartbeat. Down went Stefan, flat on his back.

Two more grabbed Mack. Their thin, delicate

fingers weren't terribly strong, so he squirmed and broke one elf's grip. But then he caught a glimpse of short clubs that looked, improbably, like bowling pins.

He had a chance to see one up close when it smashed against his nose.

"Owww!" Mack yelled. His eyes were full of tears. He knew blood was gushing from his nose. He wanted to run, but when last he checked he was on a mesa that ended in sheer thousand-foot cliffs.

Mack punched and missed, punched and missed again.

Another blow from an elfin club hit him behind the knee. The knee collapsed, and he stumbled to his left. That was lucky: he staggered out of the way of a vicious blow that just caught his ear.

The pain was intense, but the same blow hitting his head would have knocked him out.

Mack saw a dimly lit Jarrah lash out with a well-aimed kick that caught her elf assailant right where it should have really hurt.

"Ha! You know nothing of elf anatomy, you stupid, reeking sack of human secretions!"

The battle was going very badly. All four of them were either on their backs or on their knees within a few seconds. The elves weren't very strong, but there were a lot of them. Six to one. The odds were bad.

In a startlingly short time it was over. Mack was facedown with his hands and feet tied with a loop tying his bound hands to his bound feet. This bent him into a U.

A crying, angry, terrified U.

Stefan, Jarrah, and Karri were likewise hog-tied.

Meanwhile, the sun was dropping below the horizon. Soon it would be completely dark.

The elves—it was going to take Mack some time to accept that he was actually using that word—formed a little circle around them. They were as elaborately polite to each other as they had been abusive to Mack and his friends.

"What shall we do with them, brothers, friends, boon companions?" one of the elves asked.

"My own suggestion, made with utmost humility in the company of so many intelligent and experienced elves, is that we kill them."

"Would you suggest throat slitting? Or do you favor

a simple stab to the heart, wise and good friend?"

"I mention—only in the expectation of correction from my betters—that strangulation can be a solution," another elf chimed in.

The leader, if that's what he was, said, "I blame myself for perhaps not making this clear, dear brothers, but our contract with the princess requires that we make an effort if possible to deliver them alive."

"Ah, so she wishes to kill them herself?"

"No doubt, good friend. As usual, you have gone straight to the heart of the matter."

This seemed to have been a witticism, and the elves tittered politely, clapping the speaker on the back in congratulations.

Mack wasn't thrilled at the prospect of seeing Risky again. But it seemed preferable to being strangled, stabbed, or slit.

The time had come, he decided, to attempt Grimluk's magic spell once again. So he said, *"Ret click-ur!"*

That stopped the elves cold. But not because the spell worked. It didn't.

"Dare you to use the Vargran tongue against us?"

the head elf shrieked. "You worm! You pestilent malignancy! Do you imagine that you have the *enlightened puissance*? A foul, reeking toad like you?"

"Well . . . it worked once," Mack said lamely.

"Ignorant, rock-headed, jelly-jointed, brittle-limbed sputum! If you truly had the *enlightened puissance*, you would know that no spell may be reused for a period of at least one full day!"

"Oh," Mack said, crestfallen. "I didn't know that."

"Huh," Stefan said.

"I heard Grimluk use another spell, but I can't remember . . . ," Mack said to Stefan.

The name Grimluk drew a torrent of abuse from all the elves at once. They knew the name. And they were not fans.

"Brothers," the lead elf said finally, signaling an end to the heaping of insults and catcalls, "we must decide. My own small wisdom whispers to me that we must honor the princess's request and defer the killing of these mucus-smeared cretins."

There was general agreement on that, much to Mack's relief. But what they said next changed his outlook entirely.

"So, let us lower them down into the pit and seal up the hole after them."

"Wait. What?" Mack said.

"Thus will the princess find them imprisoned, entombed, but still alive."

"No. That's a terrible idea!" Mack said.

The elves grabbed Jarrah, who was squirming and trying to kick and not accomplishing much of anything. They dragged her to the hole. One of them fired up the generator that ran the winch. They dumped her into the basket. Then they did the same with Karri.

The engine strained and whirred as the two of them slid down the shaft.

Mack counted the seconds, which stretched into minutes. How far down were they?

He couldn't. They couldn't. No way.

Someone was going to rescue them because that's the way it always worked in movies. Someone would rescue him before he was buried alive, *buried alive.*

"Help!" he cried. "Heeeeelp!"

An elf smacked him on the head with his bowling-pin club. Mack's vision swam, a swirl of sunset colors tinged with the extra vibrancy of sheer panic.

He thrashed and screamed for help, head spinning, until a second blow turned out the lights.

DEAR MACK,

    I THINK SHRINKING MYSELF WAS A MISTAKE. I MADE MYSELF HALF AS BIG. DAD RAN TO TELL MOM. MOM SAID DAD NEEDED TO STOP DRINKING. THEY SOUNDED UPSET, SO BEFORE MOM COULD SEE, I WENT BACK TO MY REGULAR SIZE. THEN THERE WAS MORE YELLING, AND NOW DAD IS NOT ALLOWED TO HAVE BEER.

                    YOUR FRIEND,

                    GOLEM

Twenty-three

A REALLY, REALLY LONG TIME AGO . . .

Grimluk and the others reached the Pale Queen. And they battled her with all their powers united.

The battle raged for a day and a night.

Each of the Magnifica had his or her own areas of greatest strength. Each had mastered one of the Twelve Pairs of Potentiality. Grimluk's greatest strength was in the Birds and Animals pair. He had summoned hundreds of creatures to the battle. And many brave hawks, lions, stags, bats, wild boars, and snakes had died.

But Grimluk also had lesser abilities in Darkness and Light, and even in Calm and Storm—though that was Miladew's area of true genius.

When it was done, the Magnificent Twelve were the Magnificent Eight. Four of them had died fighting.

But the Pale Queen, at last worn down and defeated, lay pulsating, helpless, bound by spells and ropes and chains and heaped all around with the driest tinder and trusted men with torches.

The battle had been long and bloody and horrible beyond belief. It had aged Grimluk. He was no longer a young man with clear skin and firm muscles. There were lines in his face, aches in his body, a physical weakness that sometimes made breathing itself seem like labor. Worse still was the shadow that would forever darken his soul.

The castle walls had been shattered. Great chunks of wall lay scattered across the landscape. Bodies lay everywhere—on the walls, and crushed beneath remnants of the walls.

The bodies were mostly human, but there were also dead Skirrit and Tong Elves, Bowands, a scattering of Near Deads, even a pair of giant Gudridan—all of them monsters or allies of the Pale Queen.

And the destruction went beyond the castle. The entire forest had been knocked flat or burned down. Villages were gone for a hundred miles in every direction. No deer or skunk or bird or snake had survived.

Grimluk found the body of his friend the pikeman, Wick. He dug a grave for the man himself and piled stones to mark the place.

Bruise and Miladew found him standing there. Bruise had managed to upgrade his wardrobe. The one good thing that could be said for so much death was that there were now plenty of clothes to go around, although most were bloody.

"Grimluk," Miladew said gently, touching his arm. "It is time."

"The battle is over," Grimluk said. "The Pale Queen lies in chains. We won."

"The battle is over, but not the war," Bruise said.

"Drupe has called for all the wise men and witches to assemble. They will decide the fate of the Pale Queen. And we, with the last of our failing powers, must carry out the sentence."

"Surely the sentence is death," Grimluk said.

Miladew shook her head. "Nay, Grimluk. Four of the twelve are dead. To try and kill her now with what is left, with just eight, would kill us all."

Grimluk hated the Pale Queen, but this news definitely gave him pause.

Drupe stood waiting for Grimluk back at the castle. "So long as Princess Ereskigal is free, the Pale Queen cannot be killed. For at the death of the Pale One, her terrible power is inherited by her vile daughter," said the witch.

"Well, that's messed up," Grimluk said. Or words to that effect.

"She will be exiled to the World Beneath," Drupe said. "She will see no sunlight, no green plant or blue sky. She will live in the kingdom of monsters, the land of the cursed dead. Forever."

They headed back to the castle. It was wrecked, walls mostly torn down, roofs collapsed. The narrow streets were filled with bodies. In Grimluk's grim life he had never imagined he could witness anything so grim.

He wanted nothing now but to get away from here and find his family. He would take any job now, anything that would get him away from this place of horror. Anything so long as he could be back with Gelidberry and the baby he would name Victory (he couldn't quite remember whether it had been a boy or a girl).

And that's what he told Drupe when they were in the now ceiling-free and three-walled meeting chamber.

"Alas, Grimluk," Drupe said, and she laid her hand on his shoulder. "Your family is no more."

Grimluk stared at her, trying to make sense of what she was saying.

"Gelidberry and the child were in the village of Suther when it was overrun by a troop of Gudridan."

Gudridan were known for their giant size. And for their diet, which consisted almost entirely of human flesh.

"No," Grimluk gasped.

He sat down very suddenly on the cold stone floor.

He sighed deeply, and it was as if at that moment the last of his spirit left him forever. With all that he had endured, all that he had witnessed, all the pain, this pain was greater still.

Drupe squatted down beside him—a move made easier by the fact that she had managed to turn her ostrich leg into a deer's leg, which was an improvement.

"You can find a new wife. You can have a new child. You will be forever honored as the leader of the Magnificent Twelve."

Grimluk barely heard her. He just shook his head.

"The job of honored hero is yours if you wish. It pays well, and you'll be given a small farmhouse."

"I . . . I can't . . ." Grimluk began to cry, and because the concept of "macho" would not be invented for many centuries, he cried without shame.

"Those of the remaining Magnifica who so choose will scour the world searching for Princess Ereskigal," Drupe said. "So long as she lives, we cannot destroy the Pale Queen."

"I will go. The others will go with me."

"You have not very much time. As each of you ages, your powers will fade. All too soon you will be too weak to defeat the princess. And remember that the princess is not easily killed. She must die twelve deaths before she will truly be dead."

Grimluk said, "I feel like we just invented this new number twelve, and now we're using it for everything."

"Progress," Drupe said doubtfully.

"And if we fail?" Grimluk asked.

"Then there may be another future for you," Drupe said cautiously. "It would be a long, very long, but terribly lonely life."

"What could I ever be but lonely?" Grimluk whispered.

"In the secret places of the earth, in the ancient habitations of the Most Ancient Ones, death comes but slowly."

"I don't understand," Grimluk said.

"You would find such a place. And there you would live alone, cut off. You would be a sentinel. A lone watcher. You would live and wait and watch."

"Watch for what?"

"For the possibility that the Pale Queen may rise again."

Twenty-four

Mack woke too early. It was the high whine of the winch that penetrated his conscious mind.

He opened his eyes and saw . . . nothing.

"Wha . . . ?" he said.

He was aware that he was still tied up. And aware that he was facedown. On something hard. That was moving.

In a downward direction.

In the dark.

"No," he whispered.

"Be cool, now," Stefan said. His voice was from somewhere very close. Mack could feel something that might be Stefan's elbow jammed against his ear.

The truth hit him all at once. They were in the shaft. And dropping.

"Aaaahhhhh," Mack moaned.

"Dude. Relax."

"Aaaaaahhhhhh aaaaahhhhhh aaaaaahhhhh!"

See, the thing with phobias is that they aren't just regular everyday fears. They aren't even slightly more intense versions of regular fears. Phobias are like wild beasts that crouch, waiting inside your brain until something wakes them up. And once they are awake, they go crazy. Imagine a gorilla losing its mind inside a cage, beating on the bars until its paws are bloody, trying to bite through the metal until its teeth crack, slamming itself in sheer panic against walls that will break its bones.

That's a full-blown, out-of-control phobia.

And of all Mack's phobias, none was more like a crazed, penned-up gorilla than claustrophobia.

In school Mack had been required to read Edgar Allan Poe's "The Cask of Amontillado." It was the story of a man walled up and left to die. Not a happy story for anyone, but for Mack it had been agony.

And now, he was to be walled up, buried alive. So he screamed and screamed as the bucket descended. Screamed at blank, invisible stone pressing in all around him.

He was wet with sweat and hoarse by the time the lift reached the bottom of the shaft. Karri and Jarrah had already managed to free themselves from their ropes using some of the objects lying around: a pickax, the sharp edge of an open can of sardines, and a rock shaped like a wedge of cheese. Cheddar. Not that that matters.

A small flashlight waved eerily in the dark and came to focus on Mack. He felt hands busily untying the knots of his ropes. His hands and feet fell free.

He had stopped screaming but only because now the screams themselves had become frightening to him.

"So, definitely claustrophobic," Karri said with the unmistakable Aussie dryness of tone that Mack might have appreciated had he not been on the verge of vomiting.

Jarrah peered up the shaft. "No, I can't see any stars. They've blocked it."

"And the winch control is dead," Karri said calmly. "But I should be able to find some lights."

Mack saw the flashlight jerk here and there and finally settle on a bank of switches. A second later there was a click, the sound of a generator *put-put-put*ting to life, and then glaring bright light.

Mack was still shaking from the effects of his panicky meltdown. The fear was far from gone. But at least now he had a distraction to occupy some part of his brain.

The four of them were at one end of a cave so large it was impossible to see the far end, even though a row of lights had been strung from the arched roof. It was as long as a football field and almost as wide, although it was in no way regular or rectangular.

And sadly there were no bright exit signs.

One wall of the cave was lit with its own set of spotlights. It was too far away for Mack to see details, but he could see that something, lots of somethings, had been chiseled or drawn onto the rock face.

"That's what we came here to see," Jarrah said. "Can you handle it?"

Mack stood up. His legs buckled, but Stefan grabbed one arm and Jarrah caught the other and kept him from falling. On wobbly pins, stomach clenched, heart pounding but no longer quite as if it intended to beat a hole in his ribs, he walked the few dozen steps to the rock face.

The wall went thirty feet up. It was the same reddish rock that all of Uluru seemed to be made of, but this surface was polished to a near-mirror shine.

This polished area went forty feet to his left as well. And all of that square footage, a space that would equal thousands of pages of a book, was covered in what could only be writing. The letters were strange, nothing recognizable, although here and there one of the shapes would look a little like a T or a stylized Z.

The wall was scarred in places by deep fissures. In other places the rock had simply collapsed, fallen down to make a pile of pebbles and fragments.

"What is it?" Mack asked.

"We're not totally sure. But my mum thinks it's

the last ten thousand years of history," Jarrah said in a voice full of awe.

Mack looked at her, skeptical. "How could that be?"

Jarrah pointed to a series of marks that ran like the lines of a ruler across the bottom of the wall. "We think each one is a year. At the far end there's a vertical set of marks. We think those are days. And do you see these smaller markings, these curlicues? That's how I knew where you would be. We think they are sort of the equivalent of GPS numbers. Each indicates a place relative to here. Distance and angle from Uluru."

"That's crazy. I can see how maybe someone could do all this to show things in the past, but there's no way to predict what happens in the future."

"Yeah, well, that makes sense, mate," Jarrah said cheerfully. "Except for the fact that all these markings, this whole chamber, are more than ten thousand years old."

"What?"

"Mack, when this was written, all of it was in the *future*." She led him to the last chiseled inscription. It barely peeked out from the edge of a massive rock collapse, the last visible thing on the wall.

Jarrah pointed. "That right there? That's yesterday. And the curlicues? Those show distance and angle from here to the place where you fell from the sky."

"Me?"

"See that?" She pointed to an angle line with three small marks. "That's the number twelve in base four."

"Who counts in base four?"

Jarrah tilted her head and smiled mysteriously. "Someone with four fingers instead of ten, I'd guess."

"No one has . . . ," Mack said, then fell silent as a chill went all through him.

"Yeah. You get now why we wanted you to see this?"

"And what are the rays coming out of it?"

"Ah. That took a while to figure out. But then we found this." She led the way back along the wall, back into the past. They had to climb over a jumble of rocks. "See that? Same symbol. Three thousand years ago. Someone like you was here. See how the distance and angle are zero? Someone like you, Mack, one of a group of people, the Magnificent Twelve, came here, was in this place right where you're standing."

Then, with hushed reverence, Jarrah pointed to a symbol that, judging from the marks, had just appeared a few months earlier. "See that? That's a gum tree, a eucalyptus. A *jarrah*, you might say. And it is linked with you, Mack. And with the symbol for the Magnificent Twelve."

She shook her head as if she still couldn't quite believe it. "Weird, eh? To find your fate was chiseled ten thousand years ago."

Mack could only stare. It shook his entire worldview. Although in fairness his worldview had already been rather badly shaken. His worldview was a cube of raspberry Jell-O in the middle of an earthquake.

His gaze was drawn to a sort of wheel chiseled at the top of the wall. Almost like a clock, but instead of numbers there were pairs of symbols.

"What is that?"

"Ah. That," Jarrah said. "We don't quite know. I mean, we understand the symbols. They're pairs. Light and dark, speed and slowness, health and disease, and so on. We think they may be—"

"Sh!" It was Karri. "I hear something!"

There came a sound like nothing Mack had ever

heard before. It came from deep within the rock. Like something grinding its way through the limestone. Like a monster chewing rock.

"It's a pity this wall ends here," Jarrah said. "Or we might know what's happening."

"Why does it end there?"

"One of two reasons," Jarrah said. "Either it's just that the rock face shattered at this point . . ."

"Or?"

Jarrah shrugged. "Or, maybe history is coming to a sudden end."

Twenty-five

The chewing, grinding sound was getting slowly louder. "It's Risky," Mack said.

Stefan nodded. "Huh."

"Risky," Mack explained to Jarrah and her mother. "The Princess. She works for her mother. I guess it's a really weird family business."

"Risky . . . Wait! I know who that is!" Karri cried. She raced to the wall, began frantically searching it, then cried out, "There! Yes. You see this symbol, this head with too many teeth and wavy lines? It's woven all through the story, often intertwined with the female death's-head symbol.

"Ereskigal," Karri said excitedly. "Ereskigal was the Babylonian queen of the underworld. But she's known by many names. To the Greeks, Persephone. To the Norse, Hel." She grabbed Mack by his shoulders. "Are you telling me she has a *mother*?"

"That's what . . . um . . . what I hear."

Karri pushed him away. "The death's-head symbol. The mother of evil," she whispered. "I didn't understand . . . I didn't realize . . ." Eyes brimming with tears, she held her arms out for her daughter. "Oh, Jarrah. The death's-head! It's the Mother of Evil, the Breeder of Monsters. The . . . the . . . Pale Queen."

"We knew it was some great evil, Mum," Jarrah said. She was trying to sound reassuring, but Mack could tell she was shaken up.

"The old ones say she was bound for all time in the underworld, in the vast World Below. Forever!" Karri said.

"Or three thousand years, whichever came first," Mack said. "All of which is very informative, but what are we going to do about whatever is digging its way through to us?"

"I was hoping you knew," Jarrah said.

"Me?" Mack laughed, but not in a funny way. "How would I know? I only remembered that one thing I heard from Grimluk. Like some kind of magic spell or whatever, but you heard the elves: it only works once every twenty-four hours."

"It was Vargran, wasn't it?" Jarrah asked. She pointed at the wall. "That is all written in Vargran."

"We believe it's some kind of sacred language," Karri said. "A very ancient tongue . . ."

"Yeah. It's magic or whatever," Mack said. "So what can we *use*?"

"We can read it; we can't really pronounce it!"

"Give me something, anything," Mack snapped. His claustrophobia had been temporarily displaced by the fear of the princess-monster who somehow was digging through solid rock to get at him.

"I know the words for all the numbers," Karri said frantically.

"Is there a math test, Mum?" Jarrah cried. "If not, maybe something else would be better than numbers."

"I think I know how to say moon: *(sniff) asha*. And

sky: *urza*. And sun: *edras*. And we have the verb to be: *e, e-tet, e-til, e-ma*. And . . . and . . . and . . ."

"Wait," Mack said. "You can say *sun?*"

"Yes."

"And you can say *to be?*"

"There are four tenses: present, past, future, and 'or else.'"

"*'Or else?'*"

"It implies an order that must be followed or else."

"Hope my parents never learn it," Mack said. His mind was going a mile a minute. Possibly faster. "Say it. Say, 'Be sun. Or else."

"*E-ma edras?*" Karri said.

"Yes. Like that," Mack said thoughtfully.

The chewing sound was a jackhammer noise now. A crack appeared in the polished wall. Small rocks became dislodged.

"Whatever it is, it's coming straight through the wall," Jarrah said.

"I'll try to protect you," Stefan said to Mack.

"Thanks," Mack said. "And I'll try to protect you, Jarrah."

Jarrah made a dismissive snort. "I don't need

protecting." She grabbed a short steel shovel and swung it once, testing the weight. "Yeah, whoever this is, she gets it good and hard." The polished wall was shaking like an off-balance washing machine now. The noise was incredible. The wall cracked like a windshield in a car accident, star patterns racing across the rock.

Suddenly a ten-foot-diameter section of the wall collapsed. They could see a tunnel. And standing in that tunnel was a redheaded girl with lovely green eyes and massive three-pronged hands. Each prong was a shard of diamond so big it would make every diamond ever mined look like a speck of dust.

"Well, hello again, Mack," Risky said. "What a coincidence you being here."

The diamond-tipped hands were slowly melting away to be replaced by Risky's milky-white fingers dipped in blood-red polish.

Risky climbed nimbly down from the tunnel to the floor of the cave. She turned to take a look at the remains of the polished wall.

The transformation from nonchalant triumph was instantaneous. Risky's face was a mask of spite and fury. "The old meddlers," she spat.

Her blazing eyes found the clocklike symbol. "The Twelve Pairs of Potentiality," Risky said in a whisper. "Which did you think you would master, Mack? Would you like Fire and Ice? Dreams and Nightmares?" She looked over her shoulder at Mack. "Darkness and Light—I think that would have been your thing."

The diamond-tipped hands grew back in seconds. With a howl of fury, Princess Ereskigal attacked the etched stone.

The violence of it was shocking, the sound deafening. The diamond tips whirred like drills. They cut through the rock like fork tines ripping through a block of cheese.

Okay, that's not the best analogy, Mack thought. But it was close enough.

"Stop it!" Karri cried. "That is a priceless treasure!"

Her daughter, Jarrah, did not cry out. Instead she took two quick steps and swung her shovel.

It caught Risky on the shoulder.

The princess staggered to the side and spun around, fast but not fast enough. Jarrah reared back and stabbed the shovel blade with amazing accuracy. The blade hit Risky in her long, lovely neck.

The shovel bit deep.

Risky's eyes opened wide.

Jarrah drew back, determined to keep hitting until the princess was as dead as whoever had chiseled this wall ten thousand years ago.

This time Risky caught the shovel with the tip of her jackhammer hand and knocked it away.

But the damage was done. Risky's neck was sliced almost all the way through. Where blood should have gushed, a blue-black ooze, like molasses, bubbled out in sluggish spurts.

Risky's head toppled to one side. It lay on her shoulder, red hair tumbling down.

Risky's head was hanging by a thread. Her sharp hands melted to reform her own fingers. (Well, Mack assumed they were her own.)

And then, to Mack's utter horror, Risky, her head horizontal, smiled and said, "Ooooh, that pinched."

With both hands, Risky took her own head, pushed it back upright, and settled it back in place.

"Huh," Stefan said.

"Ruuuuun!" Mack screamed.

Twenty-six

A REALLY, REALLY LONG TIME AGO . . .

Grimluk wandered far and wide with his companions of the Magnifica.

Four had been killed in the great battle, so they were eight when they started out. But soon they were five. Two left for home, discouraged. Another, Bruise, was killed in a Skirrit ambush.

They buried Bruise with his wild-boar shoes and his skunk pelt.

They traveled through lands that had no name. Across seas that no one had ever crossed before. Through mountain passes clogged with snow, across waterless deserts (pretty much the only kind of desert), and along the banks of mighty rivers.

The Pale Queen might be safely imprisoned in the World Below. But her daughter was traveling the length and breadth of the world above.

Although they heard rumors of the princess here or there or somewhere else, they never caught up with her.

And with each day, Grimluk knew their powers were weaker. They were growing older and fewer in number. If they did find Ereskigal, she would be as likely to destroy them as the reverse.

Grimluk found it hard to keep going. For one thing, he and Miladew and the rest spent much of their time only looking for food. And they spent a certain amount of time fighting the evil creatures Ereskigal sent to destroy them, in addition to just random folks who didn't like strangers and thought it might be fun to stab them with spears.

But it was the death of Gelidberry and the nameless baby that weighed on Grimluk's soul.

He had been friends with Bruise, and so that death added another layer of grief.

He was sustained by his growing closeness to Miladew. She was as elegant as ever, even though she was now dressed in buttonless yak pelts and was somewhat reduced in toothiness.

From time to time they would stop and find a place to stay for a while to recover. Each of these places felt the effects of the ever-dwindling Magnifica. Eleven times they had created small camps while they tried to find a new clue to the whereabouts of the princess. Each time they left an imprint of the *enlightened puissance* behind, a mark that would be felt in the mind and soul, though perhaps not seen.

Once they chanced to return to an earlier camp and there found that others had turned the site into a sacred place.

In the end it was just Grimluk and Miladew. All the others had lost their powers, or left discouraged, or died. Just the two of them reached a far, far shore. Rumor told of a great island, the last place on the six-cornered plane of earth that they had not yet visited.

"We must find a boat," Grimluk said, gazing out at

what looked very much like all the other oceans they had crossed.

"Yes," Miladew said. "One final voyage."

"Why final?" Grimluk asked her.

Miladew sighed. "Grimluk, we have traveled together for so long a time. We have done all that Drupe asked of us and more."

"But we have not found the princess, so the Pale Queen cannot be killed."

"Grimluk, do we not have a right to some measure of our own happiness?"

"Happiness?" Grimluk echoed sadly.

Miladew then did something she had never done before. She touched Grimluk's now-scarred and sun-burned face with her now-calloused fingers.

Her touch moved him deeply, in strange ways. Feelings he had not allowed himself since the death of Gelidberry surged through his liver.

"Um . . . ," Grimluk said.

"Grimluk, the time has come for you and I to make a new life together. The past is the past. Your beloved Gelidberry is no more."

It was a thought at once frightening and enticing.

Grimluk realized just how tired he was, how much he had aged during this interminable quest.

"Happiness is not my fate," Grimluk said.

"Forget about fate," Miladew snapped. "Don't you get it? I love you, Grimluk."

Naturally this was news to Grimluk. He was a guy, after all, and not always very aware of the finer points of human interactions.

He made a grave decision then. He had told Drupe he would never give up. He had told her he would act as the sentinel, surrender all hope of a life and live in grim and terrible isolation for the rest of his days.

But the truth was, he kind of liked Miladew back.

"We will undertake this last journey, to this island of mystery," Grimluk said. "And there we shall search for the princess. But . . ."

"Yes?"

"But if she's not there, then I kind of have to think we gave it our best shot, and future generations will just have to take care of themselves. After all, the Pale Queen is bound for three thousand years. Whatever that means."

"It's a number even larger than eleven or twelve,"

Miladew said. "It is forever. Like my love for you."

Grimluk gulped.

They took a ship with a band of local folk who claimed they traveled to the island on a regular basis to hunt for the delicious *koraroo*, their word meaning "bouncing meat."

And thus, long, long ago, did Grimluk and Miladew depart for Australia, although in those days it wasn't called that.

Twenty-seven

They ran—straight into the tunnel Risky had cut. They ran like some unholy demon was chasing them.

And she was.

Karri was in front, shining her flashlight. Jarrah was right behind, with Mack crowding behind her.

Stefan had snatched up the fallen shovel and was now trotting backward, turned to face the monstrous princess.

"Back off!" Stefan yelled. "I will totally hit a girl!"

The tunnel was surprisingly smooth, but it was tubular, so the sides curved up and that made running awkward. Just the same, Mack was giving it his best.

He glanced back to see Risky just twenty feet behind Stefan. She was still holding her head on, which slowed her down a bit, particularly when she banged into the low ceiling and knocked her head straight back.

It took her a few seconds to get the head settled again.

"Ruuuun!" Mack yelled. Not that anyone needed any encouragement.

Suddenly they were out of the tunnel and tumbling across sand and through low bushes under bright stars and pale, wispy moonlit clouds. Not that Mack cared about those details.

"The buggy!" Karri gasped.

It was where they'd left it, but that was still a hundred yards away. Mack felt sharp bushes tear at his legs, and felt sand filling his shoes, but he didn't care, because he was very strongly motivated to *run* and not really worry about scratches or shoe discomfort.

"Hey, look!" Stefan said brightly. "Kangaroos!"

Sure enough, a small herd of kangaroos—although people sometimes said a "mob" of kangaroos—was bouncing along parallel with them. It made Mack feel he was moving pretty slowly because the kangaroos were quicker. They bounded, flew, and practically levitated over the ground.

Karri reached the buggy and jumped in. The rest of them piled in after her, a tangle of arms and legs, all shrieking and gasping for breath.

At which point Karri fired up the engine. The rack of lights snapped on, and there in the glow they saw Risky.

She stood there, smiling. Her head seemed to be once again firmly in place. Good for her, but not good from Mack's point of view.

The buggy lurched into gear and went tearing straight for Risky.

She sidestepped it like a bullfighter. Mack heard her laugh delightedly as they shot past.

But then the buggy was tearing across the bush, bouncing and jouncing and vibrating, and all Mack could think was, Faster, faster, faster!

He looked back and saw Princess Ereskigal

THE CALL

standing, almost a lonely figure. Then she raised her arms high, and Mack could see, though not hear, that she was shouting something.

She probably wasn't shouting, "Bye, kids! Have fun!"

In fact, she definitely wasn't, because behind Risky a storm was growing. It was like a wall of sand, as if the desert itself had come to life and was now hurtling after the fleeing buggy.

Tornadoes spawned to right and left. A howling rose, so loud it obliterated the sound of the buggy.

The storm front, that crashing wave of sand, blew and snatched Risky up with it. She was riding the storm wall like a surfer.

"Dingoes!" Jarrah cried, and pointed.

A pack of what might be yellowish wolves was vectoring to cut them off, running with what could only be supernatural speed.

But they were not alone. From every side now came the living things of the Outback. Camels, wallabies, kangaroos—all flying along the ground so much faster than nature could make them move.

Karri drove through a shrieking madness of storm

and beast, the entire Outback transformed by Risky's spell into a hammer blow that would crush the buggy and all within it.

A dingo leaped, then flew! It hit Karri from the side, right through the open window.

The buggy lurched. Karri screamed. The dingo fell into the backseat, snarling and snapping on Mack's lap.

He had time only to punch it, helplessly, before the buggy tilted and tipped and went rolling over and over. Sand and rock everywhere. The seat backs and ceiling and headrests battered Mack like he'd been tossed into a mixer set on "knead."

"Aaaahhh!" he cried.

Stefan was rolling loose inside the spinning car, knees and head and elbows punishing Mack.

Suddenly the buggy came to a stop upside down.

Mack heard crying, moaning. Stefan was stirring. The dingo squirmed. Mack tried to figure out where up was. In the front Karri was silent, still, resting upside down on the ceiling of the buggy. Her neck was at a terrible angle.

Jarrah cried, "Mum! Mum! Wake up!"

Mack pushed his way through the open window, fighting Stefan's weight. He crawled out onto the sand, still warm from the day's heat. His mouth was full of blood. His nose had been smashed earlier by the Tong Elf's club, but his arms and legs all seemed to still be working.

He rose on shaky legs to find himself standing inside a whirling maelstrom, like the calm eye of a hurricane.

The storm whipped around. The beasts waited, panting, staring wildly, doing the bidding of the evil girl who walked forward with an arrogant swagger.

"I'll bet you're ruing the day you ever listened to that old fraud Grimluk," Risky said.

"Kind of," Mack admitted.

Risky nodded. "Grimluk and his twelve were just a temporary impediment. This world belongs to my mother. And to me." She grinned her fabulous this-is-what-orthodontia-can-do-for-you smile. Then she threw back her head and laughed. "Mine! All of it, mine!"

Mack couldn't think of much to say about that, but he'd had some experience in defying bullies. "You know, there are medications that can help people like you."

"There are no people like me," Risky said.

"You're a thug, a punk," Mack said. "A murdering creep with deep mental problems. Sorry, but there are lots of people like you. Unfortunately."

"Ah, defiance. That's good: it makes it more fun. Grimluk was defiant, too. In fact . . ." She looked around, like she was trying to remember something. "Yes, it was very near this spot. No, no, wait: it was on the other side of Uluru. I remember now. Yes, that's where I killed Grimluk's little girlfriend, the next-to-last of the so-called Magnifica. I forget her name. I killed her, and I could see the way it broke Grimluk's spirit. I watched the hope die in him. Unfortunately he was able to escape. And now"—she sighed theatrically—"he's still making trouble, all these years later."

"Looks like he was tougher than you thought," Mack said. "Maybe you didn't quite break his spirit."

Risky's smile turned steely. "It's a very bad idea to fight me. You do realize I've survived for ten thousand years, don't you? I know that to you I'm just the most beautiful girl you've ever seen, but—"

"No, you're not," Mack blurted.

The smile disappeared. "You're a very bad liar, Mack. I see the truth. It's always been the truth: no male can resist me."

She came closer. And somehow, despite the howling wind, he could hear her whisper.

"Young or old, it doesn't matter," Risky said. "They all die the same way: screaming in pain. I hold the keys to the Thirteenth Pair, Mack: Life . . . and Death."

She was so close now that Mack could smell her and yes, yes, the smell of her, the colors of her hair, the slow way she blinked and then revealed again her startling green eyes, it all reached inside of him.

Took him.

"And yet, and yet . . . even as their eyes fail, and their breathing stops and their minds invent visions of welcoming lights; even as death steals their souls; even then, even as the final terror seizes them and they experience the awful silence of their own hearts, they love me."

Mack swallowed. He was frozen. Unable to move. Unable to look away.

"Have you ever been kissed, Mack?" she asked.

"No. I see that you have not. What a pity."

She touched him then, her hand on his cheek, cradling his face. "To die so very young. To die without ever being kissed."

And yes, he wanted her to kiss him. He wanted it more than he had ever wanted anything ever or could ever imagine wanting anything ever—and he was just twelve years old, so really kissing girls had not moved to the top of his agenda.

And yet . . .

Mack was vaguely aware of Karri Major stirring, waking. And of Jarrah and Stefan hauling her out of the far side of the buggy.

Risky drew him to her, unresisting. Her lips parted just slightly. She tilted her head. Her lips were so close.

A voice from a million miles away yelled, "Dude. No! Noooo!" Stefan's voice. Mack could barely hear.

From the corner of his eye Mack saw Jarrah rushing. She had something in her hand: a shovel. But she was moving in slow motion.

To his muted amazement she didn't rush toward Risky. Instead she launched herself at Stefan, hit him, carried him down to the ground.

He felt Risky's breath on his lips. He knew he would die.

Then, millimeters from her deadly kiss, Mack put his arms around her, held her close, and in a loud, clear voice cried, *"E-ma edras!"*

A small nuclear weapon went off.

Mack's body became light. And heat. Approximately 27,000,000 degrees Fahrenheit—the temperature of the sun's core.

Mack didn't feel it, didn't really even see it. It wasn't outside of him, it *was* him. The Vargran spell had turned him into a creature of blinding light and terrifying heat.

Risky's pale, soft skin and her lush red hair burst into flames.

The light lasted only a split second, but in that split second the desert was bright daylight.

Bushes caught fire.

The sand beneath Mack's feet melted to glass.

The animals nearest were incinerated. The rest turned and ran, blinded, panicked.

The gas tank of the buggy exploded.

But mostly, Risky burned. She staggered back, a living torch.

The storm ended in a shower of falling sand.

Risky screamed in pain but much more in rage.

She pointed a flaming, crisping hand at Mack. "You!" she screamed. "You!"

And then, Princess Ereskigal became a pillar of black, oily smoke. Her body was gone and in its place a thing of twisting, writhing smoke, and within that smoke a seething mass of shiny black insects.

Suddenly she was gone.

Gone.

"Yeah," Mack said as the killing light died out, "I think I'll do Darkness and *Light*."

DEAR MACK,

IT SEEMS A STOMACH ALONE IS NOT ENOUGH. YOU CAN'T JUST PUT FOOD IN, ALL THE TIME. ANYWAY, MINE BECAME TOO FULL AND I NEEDED A WAY TO GET THE FOOD OUT OF MY BODY.

DAD'S POWER DRILL WAS VERY USEFUL, MUCH BETTER THAN A SPOON.

YOUR FRIEND,
GOLEM

Twenty-eight

A REALLY, REALLY LONG TIME AGO . . .

Grimluk left the island continent after the death of Miladew.

He had failed to kill the princess. And so long as she lived, her mother, the Pale Queen, must live as well. She at least was bound for all eternity. Or three thousand years. Whichever came first.

Well, it turned out that three thousand years was not eternity.

He remembered it all still.

His body had rotted. His powers had faded. But he still remembered Gelidberry. And the baby. He even remembered the cows. And he remembered Miladew, murdered by Princess Ereskigal.

Of the long, long walk to his final home, the lightless cave where he had remained ever since, he remembered only a little.

Grimluk no longer remembered the spot. He could not have found his hiding place on a map.

But he remembered those he had loved.

And now, with evil once more rising from its foul World Below pit, he would strive with all his power to take his revenge and do all he could to guide the new Magnificent Twelve to ultimate victory.

Then, and only then, could Grimluk allow himself the peace of death. . . .

Twenty-nine

It was many hours before the ambulance came and took a battered and injured Karri away to the hospital in Alice Springs.

At the hospital Mack's broken nose was bandaged. And the strange sunburn that Stefan and Jarrah had suffered despite being in the lee of the overturned buggy was covered with salves.

Karri would be in hospital (as they say in Australia) for at least two weeks. Jarrah promised she would call her father and go with him to somewhere safe.

But once outside the hospital room, Jarrah looked at Mack and said, "Okay, where to?"

"What do you mean?" Mack asked. "You're going off with your dad."

"Like fun, I am," Jarrah said. "We're the Magnificent Twelve, right? I only see two of us, plus Stefan." Actually, she didn't see Stefan just then because he was in the men's room.

"Jarrah, we almost got killed. And I don't think we're done with her. Or the Nafia or the Tong Elves or the Skirrit or—"

"No, we're not done," Jarrah said grimly. "Not by a long shot. So I'll ask again: where to?"

Mack took a deep, shaky breath. He missed home. He missed his parents. He felt terribly alone in some ways, but at the same time he was beginning to see himself as part of a history that stretched a long way back—maybe for eternity. Or at least three thousand years.

And there was the fact that he didn't want to live in a world dominated by Risky. Or her mother.

Well, he thought (wrongly as it turns out), at least Risky's done for.

"I don't know where we go next," Mack admitted.

Which was when Stefan strode up. "Yo. Dude. In the men's room toilet, there's a call for you."

Princess Ereskigal took some time to rebuild herself after the burning. It was unpleasant and time-consuming. It was hungry work, too. She called for and ate two of the Tong Elves. After all, if they had done their job . . .

She had suffered one death. In all her long, long life, Risky had never suffered a death. She still had eleven lives left, but eleven, as even the ancients knew, was not as big a number as twelve.

Hanging over all her thoughts was the realization that she would have to go to her mother and explain that she had failed.

There were times when Risky really didn't get along all that well with her mother. It wasn't easy being the chief spawn of the Breeder of Monsters. Sometimes Risky envied girls who were the daughters of the Mother of Cheerleaders or the Mother of Pop Stars.

Living up to all those high expectations, having to be the perfect, distilled essence of evil? Sometimes

Risky just wanted to be a normal girl.

No, not really. Are you kidding? What, and ride a bike to school every day? Learn algebra? Date middle-school boys? Please.

Once Ereskigal had put her beautiful self back together, she summoned her personal flying craft, climbed aboard, and headed for the closest portal to her mother's underground lair and prison.

Before she got there, she knew she'd better have a plan. The Pale Queen, her mother, was not sentimental. She, too, sometimes ate those who had failed her.

Risky looked at her reflection in the black glass as she raced through the stratosphere at supersonic speeds and thought, I could hardly blame her; I would be a tasty snack.

Mack. He was the key. Take him out of the game now, before he could rally any more of the twelve. A simple killing now. Or war later, with consequences that no one could foresee.

"I missed you once, Mack of the Magnificent Twelve," Risky vowed. "The next time you'll be my dinner."

The Golem was sent home from school with a message for Mack's parents. The message was from Mack's school adviser, Mr. Reed.

The message read:

RICHARD GERE MIDDLE SCHOOL

Dear Mr. and Mrs. MacAvoy,

This is going to sound crazy, but three different students report seeing Mack remove his hand and attach it to the side of his head. They say he did it as a joke. And of course we know Mack didn't actually remove his hand and attach it to the side of his head and then proceed to use it to feed himself popcorn. But it sure looked real on the security camera tape. Anyway, I felt you should be made aware, especially coming on the heels of the now-infamous fart balloon incident. Any more bizarre and disruptive behavior from Mack and I'm afraid we may have to consider transferring him to the Arizona School for Excitable, Disruptive, and Unmanageable Pupils.

Tom Reed

The note was puzzling to the Golem as it seemed to indicate there was something wrong with relocating various body parts. And he was very concerned about this transferring thing. Mack would almost certainly be upset to find himself enrolled in a different school.

This was not something he felt he could manage on his own. He needed Mack's advice if he was going to avoid trouble.

Which was why Mack received a text message that read:

> Sup Mack? ☺ Im GR8 FYI. I no u r busy/dead but IMHO Mr. Reed H8 me. ☹ Do you want 2 go to ASFEDUP? BTW what is bizarre & disruptive behavior? Can u make me a list? Yr BFF. Golem.

Fortunately for Mack's peace of mind, he did not get this text before climbing on the flight to China.

The flight from Sydney to Shanghai was long. And since even a quick glance at a map will show you that there's quite a bit of ocean between Australia and China, you know that Mack spent most of the flight gripping the armrest, sweating, and muttering under his breath like a crazy person.

Stefan spent the time thinking about . . . okay, he didn't really think about anything. He played the video games in the seat back. Then he watched movies. And at one point he socked Mack in the jaw, but only because Mack's panicky weeping was causing a little boy across the aisle to start crying, too.

Jarrah cried a little as well, but for different reasons. Her mother and father had not wanted her to go. And having now seen just a little of the evils ahead, Jarrah wasn't so sure she wanted to go, either.

But that's the thing about saving the world: when the call comes, you pretty much have to answer.

At least you do if you're one of the Magnificent Twelve.

Craving more heroics?